Rebecca S. Clarke

Jimmy Boy

Rebecca S. Clarke

Jimmy Boy

ISBN/EAN: 9783337409487

Printed in Europe, USA, Canada, Australia, Japan

Cover: Foto ©Andreas Hilbeck / pixelio.de

More available books at **www.hansebooks.com**

LITTLE PRUDY'S CHILDREN

JIMMY BOY

BY

SOPHIE MAY

AUTHOR OF "WEE LUCY" "LITTLE PRUDY STORIES" "DOTTY DIMPLE
STORIES" "LITTLE PRUDY'S FLYAWAY SERIES" "FLAXIE
FRIZZLE SERIES" "THE QUINNEBASSET SERIES" ETC.

LEE AND SHEPARD PUBLISHERS
10 MILK STREET
BOSTON

TO

MASTER EDMOND H. MORSE

OF

BALTIMORE

CONTENTS

*

JIMMY-BOY

I

THE pepper-tree in the backyard nodded
its long, sweeping branches as if it were in-
viting the little white burro to come and
stand in its shade.

The burro was coming, with Jimmy-boy on
his back and the dog Punch at his heels.

"Selim is always glad to get home," said
John, the coachman, as he helped Jimmy-boy
down, and fastened the burro to the pepper-
tree.

" Yes ; he likes to switch flies," said Jimmy, patting Selim on the shoulder.

Jimmy was a fine, straight boy, with frank

9

brown eyes and a pleasant smile. People
called him "a noble little fellow;" and so he
was on the whole, but he admired himself
rather too much. It was hard for him to
own that Jimmy Sanford Dunlee ever did
anything wrong. You will see this for your-
self as we go on with our story.

Jimmy-boy and Punch ran along to the
garden at the left of the house. Here was
a little pond with a stone wall around it.
It had been made there just to look pretty;
and water went into it from a long pipe
that lay under the ground.

Jimmy paused to converse with a horned
toad sitting half hidden under a black calla.
There were three or four horned toads near
the pond, all brought there by Jimmy-boy;
but this was the youngest, and his especial
pet. Jimmy had more than once saved the
gentle creature from being pounced upon by
Judy, the cat.

"I won't let Judy get you if I can help it, Jacky Horner. But if she comes, you must hook her with your little horns, Jacky. Now mind what I say!"

Jacky's black eyes glistened like two round beads. He did not try to run away or hide; for he had learned that this small boy who fed flies to him was his friend.

As Jimmy went toward the front veranda, he heard a pleasant child-voice singing from somewhere up in the air, —

"My bonnie sweet Jamie is all my joy."

The voice was wee Lucy's, and she was singing a Scotch song which had been taught her by her sister Kyzie. But where was Lucy? Jimmy looked up to the tower windows, but could see nothing of her.

"Where are you, Lucy?"

"Up here," she answered.

"Up where?"

"Up in the sky."

He looked again, and beheld his little sister sitting high on the limb of a tall cypress-tree. How had she got there? Jimmy was startled; for it was all of a quarter of a minute before he saw Mr. Henry Sanford, who had hidden, laughing, behind the tree. The young man had raised Lucy to her lofty seat, and was now standing guard over her.

" You never knew your little sister had wings, did you, Jimmy-boy?" said he.

" I'll have 'em when I go up to heaven," cried Lucy, " and I'll fly this way!" spreading out her little skirts, and waving her arms above her head.

It was well that Mr. Sanford was there to catch her before she fell.

" There! I wanted to get down awf'ly!" she cried, as she landed on the grass. " I *fink* that pie is done."

" The Washington-pie," explained Jimmy

to Mr. Sanford. "It's just a cake with jelly in. I don't know why folks call it a pie. Vendla is making it for George Washington ; it's his birthday to-morrow."

"Aren't you a little mistaken there, Jimmy? To-morrow will be Fourth of July, not Washington's Birthday."

"Oh, wasn't he born to-morrow? I thought papa said so," said Jimmy, slowly following Lucy, who had gone in search of the pie.

She had already bounded in at the back door, and, finding no one in the kitchen, had danced along to the pantry. There it was on the shelf by the window. Not a pie, —a lovely, plump brown cake. Some people were coming visiting to-morrow, perhaps a good many people, and Washington with them. That was the reason the cake was so very large, Lucy thought.

Was it cooling properly? The child hopped about, making little exclamations, and thinking

Washington would like his cake, it was so
large and brown, and so slippery smooth.

"Tastes like choc-lid drops, I s'pose. No;
like candy-mels. Wish I knew how it does
taste." She gazed and gazed. "Would mamma
care if I should touch it with my finger, —
so, — my littlest finger, just to see 'f it's
hard? *I* wouldn't hurt it any! Why, it's
just as soft!"

Delightful discovery! And, being soft, a
scrap of it adhered to that littlest finger.
Only a *tiny* scrap. And pray, what could
Lucy do but put it in her mouth?

"'*Tis* like choc-lid drops. No; I don't know
— maybe it's like candy-mels. Can't tell
'thout I have a bigger piece."

The first hole had been no deeper than
the dimple in Lucy's cheek; the next hole
went farther in. She was ready for the third
nibble when her brother entered the pantry.

"Lucy Lyman Dunlee!" he exclaimed;

"that's a Fourth o' July Washington-pie! Made for company! Now you'll catch it!"

"I wasn't hurting Wash'ton's Fourthy July pie; 'course I wasn't," returned the little mischief very innocently.

"I never saw such a girl. You're as bad as the captain's monkey," said Jimmy severely. But he was not looking at Lucy; he was looking at the pie. "Go right away and let it alone! I suppose you don't mean to go, though. Why, how you *have* dented it up!" Here Jimmy seized a knife, and made a neat little dash at the frosting. "There, *that* doesn't leave any mark."

A large bit was left on the knife, a much larger one than Lucy had been able to secure. She opened her mouth expectantly; but, strange to say, the dainty morsel went straight into Jimmy's own mouth, not hers!

"Hello! that's good," said he. "I don't like frosting after it's all dried up."

"Nor me, either! Give *me* some!" pleaded the little sister.

"There, take that; I'm only smoothing it off. You were a naughty girl to touch it in the first place. Maybe when you get as old as I am you'll have some sense. You see," he added, as he went on making repairs, "I *have* to smooth it off, or mamma'll know what you've done, and you'll get a snipping."

It was very interesting business "smoothing it off;" it gave the children so many chances to find out just how the frosting tasted.

But alas! Jimmy's knife made worse havoc than Lucy's finger had done. Though he tried his best, it would leave deep tracks like a wagon-wheel in the mud. Or you might have fancied a dozen mischievous brownies had been driving over that beautiful cake pell-mell on their bicycles.

Jimmy, amazed and alarmed, gave it up at last.

"No use," said he. "For shame, Lucy Dunlee!" and hid the "Fourth o' July Washington-pie" behind a pan, there to dry in all its ugly roughness.

Vendla descried it that afternoon, and showed it to her mistress. Vendla was the new girl, a Swede, who had come after Molly was married.

Mrs. Dunlee summoned Jimmy-boy into the pantry, and pointed out to him something which looked like a huge mud-ball baked in the sun. It was the ruins of the Washington-pie. Jimmy was deeply mortified, but tried to defend himself.

"'Twas Lucy began it, mamma. True's the world, 'twas Lucy! *Boys* don't do such things. She pitched right in and spoiled it, or I wouldn't ever 'a' touched it."

"James!" said his mother sternly.

"I only tried to smooth it off, mamma, so folks wouldn't know folks had touched it. If Lucy " —

" So because Lucy had picked off some of the frosting, you must meddle with it too. And now you throw all the blame on your little sister ! How shabby of you ! Isn't my boy any more manly than this ?"

Jimmy hung his head. It was dreadful not be a manly boy. He scowled at the cracks in the floor, and thoroughly despised himself.

"I don't see," moaned he, laying his hand with a gesture of despair on his chest, "I don't see how such mean things get into my " — he paused, unable to think of the right word — "into my — stomach."

He meant his *heart*.

" I'm older'n Lucy is, and I'm a boy. She's only a girl ! I think I was mean, awful mean, mamma ! "

It was a great thing for Jimmy to own this. "Well said, my son! I like that. But you know you are apt to forget. You forgot twice last week to be manly toward Lucy. Is there any way to make you remember?"

Jimmy's hand, which had been pressed upon his heart, dropped suddenly. He hoped his mother would not think it necessary to punish him very much.

"If — if you don't let me eat any of that Fourth o' July Washington-pie, mamma" —

"Certainly I shall forbid the pie at any rate, because you meddled with it. But now for being a coward, and saying, ''Twas Lucy;' what ought we to do about *that*?"

"O mamma, mamma!" cried Jimmy in alarm, "you wouldn't take away my fire-crackers and pin-wheels and things? — you wouldn't do it, mamma?"

"My precious boy! I couldn't bear to deprive you of the beautiful rockets and Roman candles which Mr. Sanford and your papa have given you for the Fourth! There must be some easier punishment; let us think."

Jimmy looked relieved.

"Didn't Aunt Vi give you some money to spend for candy?"

"Yes, mamma; two bits," (twenty-five cents). "But I want it! Gilly Irwin is coming in the morning to go to the candy stores with me. O mamma, please!"

"But, my dear, if I should pass by your faults you would forget them, and then you wouldn't improve. I really think you ought to go without your Fourth of July candy."

"Oh — Oh — Oh!"

"I shall not take away the money; however. You may simply drop it in your bank."

Jimmy twisted his neck and twirled his fingers, but said not a word.

Two people in this world were always right,

he thought, — mamma and papa. Always right, and never changed their minds; so it wasn't of the slightest use to tease.

But Fourth of July, and not a speck of candy! Oh, dear!

II

SEVEN PEPPERMINTS

GILBERT IRWIN appeared at Mr. Dunlee's next morning, holding in his hand a tiny lizard-skin purse, containing a dime and a nickel.

" Come, Jimmy," said he; " let's go get our candy."

Before Jimmy could answer, the Chinese vegetable man, Quon Wo, drove up to the back door, calling out in a high, squealing tone, —·

" Platoes, *sleet* corn, cabbagee, spinny-gee!"

" What's a spinny-gee? Give us a spinny-gee!" laughed both the boys, running up to Quon Wo, whom they knew very well.

" Go 'way! Too much, talkee, talkee ! "

replied the Chinaman, grinning, and show-
ing nearly all his white teeth. At the same
time, being ready for a frolic, he pelted both
the boys with a handful of spinach.

Vendla stood in the doorway with a basket
and a pan. She bought potatoes and celery.
These went into her basket, and then she
held out the pan for something else.

Quon Wo knew what she wanted. He had
promised her some nice fresh ducks' eggs ;
and there they were, under the seat of the
cart in a pretty tea-chest.

" Duckee ! Duckee ! " said Quon Wo.
" Duckee heap good ! " and counted out the
eggs into her pan, twelve of them, and then
drove away.

The boys would have run after him, but
Jimmy happened to remember why the ducks'
eggs had been spoken for. John wanted to
put them under a hen, to be hatched into
ducklings. And here came John, carrying in
his arms a white hen, squawking angrily.

"Oh, yes, you must, Polly White; yes, you must!" said John. "You've been wanting to for a good while, and now we're ready for you. Come, Vendla, bring on your ducks' eggs."

Vendla went to the stable with the pan; the little boys, the dog Punch and his friend Toby, Mrs. Porter's dog, close at her heels. After the eggs had been put in a nice nest of straw, John placed Mrs. White over them, covering her up with a basket.

"Now stay there," said John, "and see how you like it."

Polly was very young, and had never sat on any eggs before. She had thought it would be good fun; but when the basket was put over her, she felt as if she should fly. It was not pleasant to be shut up in the dark.

"How long will she have to stay?" asked Gilbert.

" Four weeks. 'Twill be easy keeping count ; four weeks from Fourth of July."

The words " Fourth of July " reminded Gilbert that he must buy his candy.

" Come, Jimmy," said he, shaking his purse up and down. He liked to hear the coins jingle. " Where's your purse, Jimmy ? "

Jimmy drew out of his pocket a small, very pretty mother - of - pearl portemonnaie, and sighed as he opened it. It held a nickel and a one-cent stamp.

" I can't buy any candy to-day ; but you can buy yours all the same."

" Why can't you ? "

" 'Cause I can't."

"Oh, ho ! been a bad boy ? "

" Not much ; not very ; no ! "

Then, as Gilly jingled his money again, Jimmy added rather tartly, —

" Not half so bad as you are, Gilly Irwin ! "

" Me ? Who said I's bad ? "

" Well, you are; but your mamma doesn't know it, and that's why you don't be punished."

Gilly whistled. Perhaps he felt that there was some truth in this.

" Your mamma punishes *you* more'n you are naughty," he said.

" Now you stop!" cried Jimmy. " My mamma always finds out things. She isn't talking all the time with ladies in the parlor, the way your mamma is."

" Pshaw! You think you have the best mamma and best papa and best everything!" exclaimed Gilly.

" So I have!" said Jimmy confidently.

This was more than even the mild-tempered Gilly could bear.

" *What* you mean? My papa is a major, and yours isn't!"

" H'm! My papa doesn't want to be a major, and that's why! Some people *perfers* to be ministers!" Jimmy's eyes were growing fiery. "Don't you know," he went on, "ministers are the nicest men there is in this world?"

But Gilly refused to be crushed.

"Has your papa got a coat with gold cushions on the shoulders, Jimmy Dunlee? Does he go march, marching, when they beat the drum?"

"No; he just despises to go march, marching! He stays in his pulpit, I s'pose you know!"

The foolish dispute might have gone on much longer if Gilbert had not changed the subject by saying, —

"I want some cocoanut taffy."

But Gilly's "candy-man" was away that morning. He had just started with his wife and children for a picnic.

Jimmy did not care very much.

"See the folks, lots and lots of 'em, going to Fourth o' July," said he. "You can't get any candy to-day, Gil Irwin."

"Yes, I can. I know where I can get some, better'n *you* ever saw. There are some new ladies in that yellow house by the corner that sell it. I went there the other day with mamma, and got some."

"Let's go there, then," said Jimmy.

They turned into a quiet street, and walked three or four blocks, till they came to a pretty buff cottage half covered with roses.

The "new ladies," — really quite old ones, — had lately bought it to live in; and of course it was not a shop, and they kept nothing to sell. Only, as it happened, they had given Gilly a cake of maple-sugar the Thursday before, when he called there with his mamma.

"It doesn't look a bit like a shop," said Jimmy, as they walked up to the front door of this quiet house, and Gilly pounded on the screen-door. There was an electric bell at the side. Jimmy did not think candy-shops generally had electric bells. It was too late, however, to turn back.

A sweet old lady came into the hall, looking rather surprised. She naturally thought that only rude children would pound in this way for admission; yet these boys did not look rude nor disrespectful.

"How do you do, my dears? Oh, this is Gilbert Irwin, I think. But whom have you brought with you, Master Gilly?"

"My name is James Sanford Dunlee," replied Jimmy, bowing low, hat in hand.

"Ah, yes, the minister's son. I'm glad to see you both. Please walk in."

Gilbert entered, followed slowly by Jimmy.

"Can you sell us some candy, ma'am?" asked Gilly in a low voice. It was dawning upon him that he had made some mistake.

"Candy? Did you think I kept it to sell?"

Mrs. Alvord smiled as she asked the question. She was a gentle, graceful lady, all in black. She had been putting on her bonnet when the children knocked, and had not finished tying the strings.

"I don't keep candy to sell. You've come to the wrong place, my dears."

"Oh!" said Jimmy.

"Oh!" echoed Gilly, gazing regretfully at his portemonnaie. He had kept it all the while in his hand.

"Have you been trying to buy candy?"

"Yes, ma'am," answered Gilly; "but the candy-men 'most all have gone off to Fourth o' July."

"What a pity!" said Mrs. Alvord. "I wish I had some candy for you."

"Come, Gilly," whispered Jimmy, plucking his companion by the sleeve. "Come, Gilly; let's go."

"Wait a minute," said Mrs. Alvord. "My sister, Mrs. Lewis, keeps peppermints sometimes in a box on her bureau. Now, if peppermints will only do?"

She had turned to go up the staircase. Jimmy felt that it was not polite to give the kind lady all this trouble; but before he could think exactly what to say, or indeed whether he ought to say anything at all, she was gone.

• She soon returned, bearing in her hand a pretty gilt-edged plate, on which were several peppermints, pink and white.

"Just fourteen. I'm so glad there were any left!" said she, smiling. "Mrs. Lewis wishes she had a boxful. Now hold out your hands, little boys, and I'll divide. Seven for you, Master Gilly, and seven for you, Master Jamie."

Gilbert had opened his lizard-skin wallet by this time, and was offering Mrs. Alvord first the nickel, and then the dime.

"No ; oh, no ; keep your money, child! I
give you the peppermints."

And she put half of them in his hand. He
dropped purse and coins on the hall carpet,
and for a minute forgot to say " Thank you."

" And here are yours, Master James."

But James did not hold out his hand.

" Don't you like peppermints ? "

" Yes, I thank you."

" Then why not take them ? Gilbert has
had his share."

Jimmy dropped his eyes to the black ruffles
on the lady's skirt, then turned shyly away.
Must folks *always* answer folks' questions?
Yes ; he had been taught that they must.
So, in a low voice, but, as I think, very
bravely, he replied, —

" Mamma told me not to buy any candy
to-day."

" He's been a naughty boy," struck in Gilbert, who certainly might have kept quiet.

Mrs. Alvord looked from one boy to the other, her glance resting at last very kindly on Jimmy.

"But, my dear, you are not, *buying* this candy; it is given you."

Still Jimmy did not reach forth his hand.

",Ah! you really think you ought not to take it? Then don't do it by any means. You are a noble, manly, little boy, James Dunlee."

Jimmy blushed for pleasure, but could not raise his eyes. Oh, wasn't it grand to be called a manly boy!

"You may have been naughty once, but you are good now, and I shall tell your mamma so. I'm going to your house to dinner."

Jimmy's little face was radiant. Mamma would know he was manly after all!

"And now shall I give the rest of the peppermints to Gilbert?" asked Mrs. Alvord.

Gilbert took them eagerly, wondering why

Jimmy had refused them, and suspecting that Jimmy did not care much for peppermints.

"That's the 'Jimmy-boy' the blind Mrs. Pope talks so much about. He is a boy to be proud of," said Mrs. Alvord, as she finished tying her bonnet-strings before the glass in her sister's room.

"Dear little fellow!" returned Mrs. Lewis, "I am so glad I shall see him to-day."

III

FOURTH OF JULY

ALL this while wee Lucy was growing impatient.

"I fink Jimmy might come back," said she.

For she had a small tricycle, and he was teaching her to ride.

"When will he come, Vendla?"

Vendla did not know. She thought he might come by ten o'clock.

"Well, what's *now* o'clock?"

"It's half-past nine o'clock now."

Lucy ran to the back parlor, and climbed a chair that stood by the mantel. The pretty marble clock was ticking its best; but she thought it did not tick fast enough. She opened the door of the clock, and moved the black hands round.

"Now maybe 'twill strike," she thought; "and then he'll come."

It did strike, again and again, and yet again, till the sweet cathedral chimes filled all the air, and mamma came hurrying down-stairs to see what had happened.

"Lucy, Lucy," said she in a tone of displeasure, "have you been touching the clock?"

"I *had* to make it strike, mamma, so my Jimmy would come," replied the little rogue, scrambling down from the chair. "Are you *in earnest*, mamma? Oh, I don't want you to be in earnest with your little girl!"

She looked in her mother's face anxiously as she spoke; and Mrs. Dunlee promised to forgive her if she would never meddle with the clock again.

"No, I won't ever, mamma, ever any more."

At that very moment Jimmy appeared.

Lucy ran up to him, laughing and crying; laughing because she had brought him home by making time go faster ; crying because mamma was "in earnest" with her little girl.

" I'm all ready, and my dolly's been all ready for ever 'n' ever. 'Most got the friz out of her hair," said Lucy reproachfully.

The brother and sister had a long ride, each on a little tricycle ; and Punch, who was in attendance, could not have been prouder of his little master and mistress if they had owned the whole State of California and part of Mexico.

Jimmy usually reproved Lucy for "doddlin' round and wiggling so ;" but was very patient to-day, and said, " You do *pretty* well — for a girl ! Sometimes you do go so awful slow that it tires me all out to keep up with you. Now see *me !* "

And away he spun alone on his little wheel,

his sister gazing after him in wonder, admiration, and despair.

They had both planned to give the baby a " Fourthy July" ride in his own private carriage, to the tune of, —

> " Yankee Doodle came to town
> On a Kentish pony ;
> Stuck a feather in his hat,
> And called it Maccaroni."

But objections were made to this. Eddy was young and tender, and could not stand the jolting.

" H'm ! *boys* can stand 'most anything," said Jimmy. "You'd think he was a girl, to hear 'em talk ! "

" Glad he isn't," returned Lucy, patting baby's cheek. "I want him for a little brother. What do I want of a little sister ? *I'm* a little sister *myse'f !* "

It was time now for dinner. There were two guests in the parlor, Mrs. Alvord and

Mrs. Lewis. As Mrs. Alvord took Jimmy-
boy's hand, she said, —

" May I kiss you on your cheek, Master
James ? You don't know how I wanted to
kiss you this morning ! "

Jimmy offered both cheeks with a blush
and a smile. He was proud and happy to
be admired by this sweet lady ; and he was
sure, too, that she had told, or was going to
tell, his mamma all about his call at " the
yellow house by the corner " with Gilly
Irwin.

" I am glad to know you too, Master
Jimmy-boy," said Mrs. Lewis, a tall lady
with tiny white curls about her face. " Mrs.
Alvord and I love little children ; but we have
none at our house, and your mamma has five.
I'm going to ask her if she can't spare *us*
one, — you or Lucy or the baby. Which
do you think she would give away ? "

Jimmy knew very well by the twinkle in

the lady's eye that this was only said in
sport. He reflected a moment, then replied, —

"It's polite to give away the largest pieces
and things ; so I think mamma ought to give
me !"

Both the ladies laughed, and thought this
a bright answer. Jimmy felt rather proud
of it himself, and looked around to see if
mamma had heard it. But Mrs. Dunlee was
not in the parlor.

She had stolen into her husband's study
just for a moment, to tell him Mrs. Alvord's
story of Jimmy-boy.

"A small thing, to be sure," said she ; "he
only gave up seven peppermints !"

"*Not* a small thing, my love," returned
Mr. Dunlee. "It shows that the boy has
character. I am as happy about it as you."

Jimmy thought it a remarkably pleasant din-
ner-party. There was maccaroni soup, which
reminded Lucy at once of the singular sort

of feather which "that Yankee Doodle boy" had stuck in his cap.

"This is Yankee Doodle soup!" said she in a loud whisper to her brother, who nearly choked from trying not to laugh.

Sister Kyzie scowled darkly. When would Lucy learn not to whisper at table? How often must she be told to move her spoon away from, and not towards, herself in taking soup?

When the dessert came on, strange to say, it was that same "Fourth-of-July-Washington-pie," no longer brown and ragged, but shining as white as the far-off mountains at Christmastide. What had Vendla done to it? And why did mamma smile every moment? Was she thinking how much fairer the great cake looked now in this creamy covering? Jimmy knew she was not thinking of the cake!

After dinner he entertained Aunt Vi and

Mr. Sanford on the veranda by firing off a round of crackers.

"Jimmy, Jimmy!" pleaded his aunt at last. "If you'll only be quiet a moment, I'd like to show you something."

She opened an old book, and he and Lucy drew near to look at the picture of a man in a military coat and cocked hat.

" I know who that is!" exclaimed Jimmy; " that's George Washington ! "

" Right," said Mr. Sanford; "the very man you said Vendla made the pie for. And who was he ? What did he do ? "

"What did he do?" repeated Jimmy. "Why, I know that just as easy ! "

Then, after a long pause, —

"Well, anyway he had a hatchet. No, no," seeing an amused look on Mr. Sanford's face; "'twas when he was little that he had the hatchet ! But afterwards he was — was he the president ? "

"Yes ; our first president."

Then Mr. Sanford told as simply as possible what the good man did for us more than a hundred years ago to make us a free nation.

Jimmy listened carefully, and understood a little of it. He was glad to learn that we are free.

"I like to be free," said he, swinging his arms and throwing out his chest. "I like to have a president ruling over me! Not a queen, you know, away off in England! That would be awful! Why, we should have to sail to England in a ship every time we wanted to ask the queen a question!"

"But here is little Lucy," said Mr. Sanford, "who looks as if she cares very little about kings and queens. Perhaps she would like to hear the story of the hatchet."

Then he took her on his knee, and told her how the little George Washington long,

long ago had the present of a hatchet, and enjoyed swinging it so well that he cut down a small cherry-tree before he stopped to think.

Lucy was very indignant. She loved trees, and often stood and gazed up at them with awe and delight. She was always angry when she saw a man cut off the tops of eucalyptus trees, even though she knew it was done to make the trees grow broader and handsomer.

"Georgie was a naughty boy," she said. "I don't like Georgie!"

"But," said Mr. Sanford, "I told you how sorry he was. Don't you think children should be forgiven when they are sorry?"

"I do," returned Jimmy; "'specially when they *can't tell a lie!*'"

Still Lucy was pitiless.

"They won't have any more cherries at that boy's house — *ever!*"

And slipping down from Mr. Sanford's knee

she strode into the house without looking
back.

Mr. Sanford was sorry he had told her the
story.

"She doesn't care much if George Washington *couldn't* tell a lie," said Jimmy. "All
she cares about is the cherries."

"Perhaps she thinks," remarked Aunt Vi,—

> " ' If all the trees were cherry-trees,
>   And every little boy
>   Should have, like young George Washington,
>   A hatchet for his toy,
>   And use it in a way unwise,
>   What should we do for cherry-pies? ' "

After tea the whole family, with the guests,
Mrs. Alvord and Mrs. Lewis, met on the
veranda to watch the glorious sunset.

"In a few minutes we shall see the fireworks shooting up from the city," said Mr.
Sanford; "and then we'll light up our own
fireworks, Jimmy-boy, in honor of this free
country."

So saying, he made a deep bow to the American flags that hung in clusters all about the veranda.

Jimmy's eyes shone. He had lived in this free country for five years and a half, and had never known till to-day that it was free! He thought of a bird let out of a cage, of a poor wild gopher let out of a trap. What a splendid thing it is to fly or run, just as one chooses!

He looked at his treasures of fireworks lying beside him on the floor, and smiled. Ever so many boys were coming to see him send up these beautiful flaming pictures into the air. He should tell the boys, — maybe they didn't know, — he should tell them he did it because this country is free!

Wee Lucy sat on a stool with a book in her hand. She cared very little about free-dom or fireworks or "Fourthy July." She was scowling at a picture in the twilight.

" That's Georgie; that's the hatchet-man!"
said she wrathfully, and would have picked
out both his eyes with a pin if Aunt Vi had
not stopped her.

" Well, he's awful! Bad man! Bad man!
Is he alive, Auntie ? "

" No, dear ; the good Washington died long,
long ago."

Lucy clapped her hands in glee.

"Oh, I'm so glad, so glad ! "

" What ! Glad the good Washington is
dead ? "

" Yes ; 'cause now he can't come here. I
was afraid he'd come to my house with his
hatchet, and cut down some o' my trees!"

She seemed so relieved that they all laughed;
how could they help it ? But no one un-
dertook to correct her opinion of the "father
of his country."

" No use talking to her, she's such a little
goose," thought Jimmy-boy. " Wait till she's

as old as I am, and she'll know all about it."

But now the sun had fairly dropped behind the wrinkled mountains; the city fireworks had begun to play, and Jimmy's fingers were tingling to be at work on his rockets.

What a grand affair! How the neighbors, large and small, were flocking to that veranda, and with them half the dogs in town! Which rose higher and jollier, the human or the canine voices, it would have been hard to tell.

But there were silent guests too. Three horned toads sat near by, fastened by strings to three stakes. Jimmy had tied them before tea, to make sure they would have a good time " seeing the sights." They did see the sights, and their beady eyes blinked in the light; but if they had a good time they kept it all to themselves.

Whiz! Fizz! Up soared Jimmy's fireworks,

the finest ever had in town. First pin-wheels.
But that was nothing ; after that began the
real business, the grand display.

Each firework was a picture all by itself ;
and such shouting and clapping you never
heard. But last and best of all was a picture,
in gold and silver fire, of a large, grand man
in a soldier's uniform and cocked hat.

" 'Rah! 'Rah! George Washington!" shouted
Jimmy. "Take off your hats ! He's the father
of his country."

Then every hat came off, and every handkerchief was waved, till the noble figure of
Washington faded into a shower of gold-dust,
and made a path of glory along the evening
sky.

IV

WAS IT JUDY?

FOR a week or two after Polly White had begun to sit on the ducks' eggs, Lucy asked every day, —

"Where's my little duckies ? "

And then she forgot all about them.

But Polly White was still sitting. It takes only three weeks to hatch chickens; but it takes four weeks to hatch ducklings, and poor Polly did not understand it, and was growing very tired. To keep up her spirits John and Vendla gave her all sorts of nice things to eat.

At last one day the ducklings began to peck out of the shell. And when they fairly came out how funny they looked ! Very large and yellow, with round bills and yellow, flat feet ; and when they tried to walk they waddled.

Polly looked surprised. Were they all lame? Had they all sprained their ankles? She had never seen any ducklings before ; but she clucked just as proudly for all that.

"See my children! Aren't they beauties? That's a new style of walking. Isn't it sweet?"

Kyzie and Edith and Jimmy and Lucy came out to see the funny brood. Vendla set a pan of corn-meal dough near the back door. Polly was very hungry; but she would not touch one mouthful till she had called her little ones to breakfast. There were nine of them, and they dipped in their round bills like spoons.

"That's a new style of eating," clucked Polly. "Don't you admire it?"

"Do you suppose Polly White thinks those creatures are chickens?" asked Edith.

"Yes," said John, who was looking on ;

" of course she does, and very cute chickens too. You see, they belong to her."

After their breakfast they rolled up their eyes, and John said, —

" Now guess what they're thinking about."

No one could guess, and John had to answer his own question.

" They're thinking they want to swim."

" Do you believe it ? " said Kyzie. " What do they know about swimming ? They never saw any water."

There was a monstrous clay jar on the back veranda in which water was always kept cooling ; it was called an *olla* (pronounced *oya.*) But the ducklings could not have peeped into that. Kyzie was right when she said " they never saw any water."

Still these yellow fuzz-balls had made up their minds that there was water somewhere in the world, and they meant to waddle, waddle, till they found it. Nobody had ever

told them there was a pond in the garden;
but they ran that way as fast as their web-
feet could carry them. Their stepmother, Mrs.
White, ran after, anxious to stop them ; but
the moment they saw the water they tried to
go in. They could not climb up the wall.
John took them in his hands, one by one,
and dropped them into the pond.

Then they were happy. This was the very
thing they had been dreaming about as they
lay asleep in their egg-shell cribs!

But poor Polly! How frightened she was!
How she flapped her wings and squawked!
She thought her children had gone crazy;
she was sure they would drown.

No, not they! They struck out their little
feet like paddles, held up their heads, and
rowed that pond as if they were giving les-
sons in swimming. The children all clapped
their hands at the gay sight, and Jimmy
cried, —

"Cheer, boys, cheer!"

After a little, Mrs. Polly grew calmer, and
began to chuck again, —

"Those are my chickens; they're all in the
swim! See their new style of feet!"

Still she did not feel quite easy.

Just then Quon Wo, the Chinaman, drove
along, calling out, "*Sleet* corn, cabbagee,
spinney-gee."

When he found what was going on, he
shook his head till his long black cue danced
over his shoulders.

"No so!" he cried. "No *so!* Lil duckee
no slim-ee!" (Little ducks mustn't swim.)

"Why not?" said John. "See how easy
they go."

But Quon Wo still shook his cue. He
thought they ought not to swim yet without
a mother-duck who would know how to oil
their feathers for them. The stepmother hen
could not do this. "Wait till they are a

month old before they swim," was the ad-
vice of Quon Wo.

"Well, if you're going to be so fussy about
it, Quon Wo, I'll take 'em out," said John.

And he did. So the fun was all spoiled;
at least for this time.

John, Vendla, and the children went into the
house. Vendla put on her sweeping-cap, and
began to sweep the chambers, while Jimmy
and Lucy strayed off to the kitchen.

On the long table against the kitchen wall
stood an elegant china fruit-dish which Vendla
had brought out from the parlor to wash.

"Pretty dish," said Lucy, fingering the
edges lovingly.

"Let that alone, or you'll break it," said
Jimmy, in the tone of command he often used
when speaking to his little sister.

Lucy did not obey at once.

"You're the naughtiest child, Lucy Lyman
Dunlee! You'll go and break that, and then

they'll go and blame *me !* I *always* get punished for *you !* "

Jimmy pitied himself as he heard his own
words.

" Yes, Lucy Lyman Dunlee, you're the aw-
fulest acting-est child !

" If you don't stop picking cake, and spoil-
ing things, and breaking things, I'll — I'll —
why, they'll think it's *me !* and I'll grow up
to be despised ! "

Lucy sprang away from the table in alarm.
What it was to "grow up to be despised" she
had no idea. Something bad, if it made
Jimmy look like this !

" There comes Judy ! What has she got in
her mouth ? " cried Jimmy, forgetting his fear
of being "despised." " It can't be one of
Polly's chickens ? "

With that, he and Lucy began to chase the
cat about the room. Judy thought it hardly
fair to have two children after her at once, and

"Who did that?" cried Jimmy.

Page 57.

jumped into a chair, and from the chair to the table.

"She's smelling the china dish with her nose. Come down; come down!" said Lucy.

Judy did not come, but continued to sniff at the dish.

"Stop that!" said Jimmy. "Come down, or I'll pull you down!"

In a frolicsome mood he caught her by the tail, not roughly or unkindly. He had been taught gentleness to animals; but somehow in dragging her backward the fruit-dish got in the way. Perhaps Judy's paw touched it, perhaps Jimmy's elbow. Yes, it was probably Jimmy's elbow. At any rate, the dish was overturned; and as it fell to the floor it broke in half a dozen pieces.

"Who did that?" cried Jimmy in dismay. He had not been aware of touching the dish. It was certainly an accident; still he was old enough to know that he was to blame for the

accident.   He should not have played with the
cat while her nose was in the fruit-dish.

Yet he was the good boy who had just been
scolding his little sister for nothing at all!
The good boy who never did wrong!

"Oh, that beau'-ful dish!" sighed Lucy.
"Poor mamma 'll feel *so* bad!"

"Well, 'twas the cat did it," said Jimmy
quickly.

His forehead was full of wrinkles; his eyes
were full of tears.   Lucy always made ready
to cry when he cried, and now she turned up
the corner of her apron ; and for half a minute
the room was so still that you could almost
have heard a fly walking on the roller-towel.

Jimmy stood on one foot and thought : "I'll
go tell mamma I didn't mean to.   No; I'll tell
her Judy did it.   Judy did, I *think.*"

The fly on the towel gazed at Jimmy ;
Jimmy gazed at the fly.

"Mamma's pretty dish," said Lucy, breaking

the silence. Jimmy was not crying, so she
dropped the corner of her apron.

"Judy broke it," declared Jimmy again.

"Yes," assented the little sister; "Judy
broked it."

"Well — go tell mamma so. I hear her in
the parlor."

Lucy turned to go.

"No, don't; I don't want you to. Needn't
tell mamma anything."

"'No ; needn't tell her anyfing," said Lucy,
whirling about, and looking at her brother.

She and the little fly both looked at him.
Lucy did not know any more than the fly
what was going on in Jimmy's mind. Neither
of them dreamed it was a battle between right
and wrong.

"If I run out to the garden, won't that be
the best way ? Then Vendla 'll come in, and
she'll think the cat broke it. I'll shut the cat
in here all alone," thought this little soldier,

who was fighting a battle between right and
wrong.   " It will not be same as a lie, — I
think not."

Jimmy moved towards the back door, and
there he stood quite still.

Why did Lucy stare at him so, as if she
were watching to see him make up his mind ?

" Lucy Lyman Dunlee, what makes you look
so awful sober ?   Just as if papa was dead,
and mamma had been hooked by a cow ?   Why
don't you go out-doors and see — see where
Polly White is ? "

Lucy was gone in a twinkling, glad to get
away from Jimmy, who was scowling now "as
fierce as ten furies."

He looked at the door, then at the cat.
" Wish I was little like Lucy; *then* it wouldn't
be wrong.   No matter what you do when you're
little like Lucy."

Jimmy sighed.

" Babies like her ! *They* don't have to be

gentlemen. But when you're a boy, and get-
ting so big —

" Did George Washington ever shut up a
cat ? George Washington wouldn't do it. ' *I
can't tell a lie,*' says George Washington. No,
sir ! "

This seemed to settle the question for Jimmy. The ' *No, sir !* ' sounded as loud as a
cannon-ball, though even the cat did not hear.
The words were spoken only in Jimmy's
heart.

" No, sir," said he again, and ran for the
parlor as if a mountain-lion were chasing him.
He dared not walk, lest he might not go at all.

How he hated to go ! That fruit-dish was a
new one only last Christmas. Mamma would
almost cry to know it was broken.

He ran every step of the way. Mamma almost cried, it is true ; but it was just for joy !

" My blessed, blessed Jimmy-boy ! I can forgive you for carelessness ; but, oh, if you *had*

shut Judy into the kitchen, and deceived your mother ! ”

“ But I didn't do it, mamma ! ”

“ No, no, no ; God kept you from that mean-ness, the good God.”

“ Mamma, your beautiful fruit-dish is bro-ken ! ” exclaimed Edy, bursting into the parlor. “ Isn't it too bad ? ”

“ Never mind, daughter ; I'm too happy to care for such trifles,” returned Mrs. Dunlee, with a sunny glance at Jimmy that warmed him to the very depths of his heart.

V

MRS. BIDDY CHICK

When Quon Wo decided that the ducklings were old enough, they were allowed to swim. But Polly never let them go to the pond alone. She went with them, and stood on dry land, watching their graceful motions. She seemed to feel ashamed not to swim herself; but she knew there was something the matter with her feet, so she never tried to learn.

"I don't want Judy to catch any of those ducklings," said Jimmy; "Judy's horrid sometimes."

"Will Punch catch any, do you think?" asked Mr. Sanford.

"Punch!" cried Jimmy indignantly. "Punch isn't horrid; he's good."

" He's a nice shepherd dog," said Mr. Sanford, patting the animal's head. " But he's
young yet. Let me see, how long have you
had Punch ? "

" Don't you remember, Mr. Sanford ? I
should think you'd remember. 'Twas that time
I had the toothache, and Aunt Vi made some
walnut creams. It ached and ached. Mamma
said I must go to the dentist. I didn't like
to ; I was afraid. But Aunt Vi said, ' Now
you go with me, Jimmy, and I'll write and
tell Mr. Sanford.' 'Twas when you were gone.
Where were you gone, Mr. Sanford ? "

" I was at Los Angeles."

" Well, so I went to the dentist with Auntie.
She said I was brave. Boys don't cry, you
know ; not much. The thing the dentist
pulled with was as sharp as the head of a
pin, — no, the *point* of a pin. But when the
tooth came out it never ached any more after
that.

"And then Aunt Vi wrote to you ; don't you know? And you said you'd send me a present in a bag, and it would come that day to the post-office, and we must go right off and get it. I never guessed what it was ; nobody could guess.

"How I laughed! how papa laughed! It was a great, strong bag. There, turn your head round, Punch! He had a blue ribbon round his neck then. Who would have thought he came in that bag? But he did. Didn't you, Punch?

"He wasn't half as big then as he is now. He never died at all. No, Punch, you breathed all the time just the same. And when we took you out of the bag you were as alive as could be, and wanted some bread and milk."

Punch wagged his tail at this story as if he remembered it all.

"That was last March, if I'm not mistaken,"

said Mr. Sanford. " And Punch was then six months old. That would make him a year old now.

" Well, he's not very handsome, but he is a knowing dog. I think you did a good thing when you had that tooth out, Jimmy."

Jimmy's head rose a little higher.

" Well, and I told mamma I was willing to go to the dentist again, for it didn't hurt much. But mamma said I needn't go again ; 'twas no use to pull out my teeth when they didn't ache. And, besides, I don't want any more dogs, you know. What do I want of more dogs when I have Punch ?

" Punch, come here ? When you lick my hand so, and tickle me, I have to laugh. But he doesn't look as if he came in a bag, does he, Mr. Sanford ? "

Punch pricked up his ears, and began to bark. His big friend Toby across the way,

Mrs. Porter's dog, was barking, and little Punch never let Toby make more noise than he did if he could help it. Toby had espied a wagon coming up the hill. Very soon Punch saw it too through the trees, and then he knew what he had been barking about.

Dear, merry Mrs. Chick was in the wagon. She had come to town to buy her a dress, she said. And where was her little Lucy?

Lucy soon appeared on her tricycle, to the great delight of Mrs. Chick.

"I like to see the ducklings swim," she said; " but it isn't half so pretty a sight as my little girl dancing along on that fizzy-me-jig wheel with all sails flying."

Mrs. Chick wanted to take two of the children home with her to stay all night, and Edith and Jimmy were only too glad to be allowed to go.

"This time I may churn butter, mayn't I, Mrs. Chick?" said Jimmy. "You always said

I might churn butter some time in that pretty green churn."

"So you shall, if you get up early enough, my boy; so you shall," said the good-natured woman cheerily. " The cream will be all ready in the morning by five o'clock. Do you like to get up at five o'clock ? "

" I don't know. Maybe I do, if you'll call me, Mrs. Chick."

Mrs. Chick lived several miles away, on a ranch or farm. If her ranch had been all paid for she would have been a rich woman. She had lemon-trees, and a little lemon-house to dry the lemons in ; she had orange and fig and olive trees, and so many different kinds of roses that she couldn't remember all their names to save her life. The palm-trees had trunks that looked like enormous pine-apples. One queer tree with rough bark was called a " monkey-tree." Mrs. Chick said she didn't know why, unless it was because a monkey couldn't climb it !

"No," said Edy; "the needles and thorns on it would prick and scratch him awfully. I'd like to see the captain's monkey try to climb it. How he would cry!"

The young Dunlees never failed to have a good time at Mrs. Chick's. She lived alone, and had a funny way of talking to herself, and asking, —

"Do you hear what I say, Biddy Chick?"

Her first name was Bridget.

Then, too, she kept numerous pet animals, which she caressed and talked to almost like children. Somebody had just given her three bits of motherless tortoise-shell kittens; and it was interesting to see her feed them. She had a bottle of milk with a quill in it; and, taking one kitty on her lap at a time, she said, "Now, my pretty baby," and put the quill in its mouth. When the "pretty baby" had sucked all the milk that it ought to have, she put it down and took up another baby.

The beautiful little creatures were just beginning to see; and what they thought of
their large, fat mother and the bottle with
a quill in it I cannot say. But they always
ate heartily, and afterwards rolled themselves
up in little balls close together on a cushion,
and went to sleep in the sun, looking per-
fectly happy.

There was another pet, a playful young kid
with a brass collar on his neck, who trotted
about on his little black feet, following his
mistress everywhere, even into the parlor.
He, too, had been brought up on a bottle,
and his name was Trot.

Mrs. Chick had two cows, a horse, and many
hens and turkeys. She sometimes took the
turkeys with her when she went visiting.
Then there was a two years' old baby over
the way, who was always dancing in and out,·
and making a good deal of trouble; so Mrs.
Chick was seldom lonely.

The children kept thinking what a lovely time they were having; but after tea they both felt tired, and at seven o'clock Mrs. Chick sent Jimmy to bed. The chamber was unfinished, and had no paper or plaster, and in some places the ceiling was so low that even little Jimmy could hardly stand upright. There was a live-oak tree close to the window, and he had seen a bird's nest in the branches of the tree.

"I'll hear the birds singing before I wake up," thought Jimmy drowsily. "And I'll go straight to sleep, for I'm going to churn that butter in the morning."

But Jimmy did not go straight to sleep, nor did he waken early; and I will tell you why.

After he had gone up-stairs Mrs. Chick lighted a lamp and sat down in the kitchen to mend stockings, while Edith sat near her, looking over a picture-book. Presently Mrs. Chick said, —

"Dear me! I forgot to bring down that maple-sirup. I meant to have it for the waffles in the morning. But no matter now; I won't stop to go after it."

"Is it up-stairs?" asked Edith, who thought that it would be quite too bad to eat waffles without sirup.

"Yes; up-stairs in the closet in the northeast room. I keep it there because it's a cool place. I used to keep it in the pantry, but the Morse baby always found out where to look for it. She climbs everywhere."

"I think that Morse baby is more trouble than the kid," said Edith. "But can't I go up and get the sirup, Mrs. Chick? I'd like to so much."

Mrs. Chick considered. She was tired, and did not wish to go herself; but could Edy be trusted with a lamp?

"Just hand down that candle from the mantel-piece, Edy. There," said she, after lighting it, "that's safe enough! The pitcher is right on the closet floor, under the lowest shelf, behind a box. Will you be very sure not to carry the candle into the closet?"

"Oh, no, indeed! Oh, *yes*, indeed, I mean! And I'll be, oh, so careful!"

"Well, if you'll remember to set the candle down by the chamber door, I think there'll be no danger."

"Yes, Mrs. Chick, I will," said Edith, and danced away joyfully. It was almost an unheard-of thing for her to be trusted with a light, and she enjoyed it. She held the candle aloft, and peered rather cautiously about the unfinished room next door to Jimmy's. The whole house was so queer, she thought, and Mrs. Chick put things in such droll places.

"If mamma knew I had this candle she'd be nervous. She talks to me about lamps and things as if I was a baby; but I guess

she'll find out I know as much as Kyzie.
Kyzie singed her hair once. Father thinks
I can't take care. I mind all that's said to
me ; I mind beautifully.

" Now, I wouldn't forget what Mrs. Chick
told me about this candle, not for anything !
She told me to set it down by the closet
door ! "

Ah, Edith, a mistake already ! She told
you the chamber door !

" I remember a great deal better than Ger-
tie Mercer. She can't remember eight times
nine to save her life. Let's see, the pitcher's on the closet floor behind a box."

She opened the closet door, the candle still
in her hand. What a delicious odor of apricots and peaches ! Did Mrs. Chick keep her
fruit here too ? Such a funny woman !

Edith set her candle down by the closet
door, and knelt just in front of it, the bottom
of the candlestick almost touching the skirt

of her frock! But as she peered into the closet she forgot there was anything in the world but a sirup pitcher and some apricots and peaches. That candlestick with the candle in it was as far away from her thoughts, to say the least, as the moon in the sky.

But the candle did not forget. It is the duty of a lighted candle to set fire to anything that is put in its way; and presently, when Edith by a quick movement thrust her skirt right into the flame of the candle, what could you expect but a blaze?

Before Edith could explore the closet floor and take out the sirup pitcher, the blaze was creeping up the back of her frock. She knew nothing about it till the smell of burning woollen reached her nostrils; and at the same instant she felt a dreadful sensation of heat, and knew that she was on fire! She screamed in horror, —

" Mrs. Chick! Mrs. Chick! Fire! Fire!"

Oh, how far it was down-stairs ! Could Mrs. Chick hear ?

But Mrs. Chick was not in the kitchen. Feeling rather uneasy about Edith, she had followed her up-stairs, and was on the upper landing when the child called. She heard the first cry, and came at once to her aid, followed by Jimmy.

I rejoice to say that the flames had not reached Edith's hair. Mrs. Chick wrapped her in her best rug, which was quite spoiled by the means, to say nothing of the little girl's pretty red frock ; but the dear child herself was unharmed.

VI

JIMMY'S BUTTER

"DON'T cry so, you dear little girl; there is no harm done," said Mrs. Chick. "Why, Jimmy-boy! I wish you were asleep. Run right back to bed, and don't be so scared. Sister wasn't hurt a bit."

All this while Mrs. Chick, having undressed Edith, was rocking her in her arms like a baby.

"I was a naughty, heedless girl," said Edith. "I ought to have told you mamma never trusts me with any kind of a light except a taper in a tumbler. But I thought I was going to be so careful this time."

"'Twas all my fault, dearie. I knew you weren't one of the stop-to-think kind. You'll

learn by and by," replied Mrs. Chick sooth-
ingly, as she placed the trembling, exhausted
child in bed between lavender-scented sheets,
and turned to leave her.

" 'Twas all my fault," repeated the good
woman to herself. "Thank Heaven no harm
came of it! but I should think I was old
enough to know better. I'm so weak-minded
about children ; can't deny 'em anything they
ask for!

" Now, there's that cream. I've no business
to let Jimmy churn it to-morrow morning.
Something will happen to it, as sure as my
name's Biddy Chick; and I can't afford to
lose the cream. It needs a steady hand to
bring butter, and I'll do the churning myself
before he wakes up."

After this exciting adventure with the candle, it was some time before the children
could compose themselves to go to sleep. Mrs.
Chick had planned to do an unusual amount

of work next day, and wanted an early breakfast; but she had not the heart to waken
her young guests.

"Let 'em have a good rest, poor little
things! I remember how I used to hate to be
called up when I was a child; though, to be
sure, I knew I'd got to work, and that makes
a difference. Bless me! how I did have to
work!"

It was eight o'clock, and the sun was quite
high, when the children sat down to their
breakfast of omelet and waffles. The maple-
sirup had been forgotten after all, and Mrs.
Chick had to go up-stairs for it.

"I've saved the cream for you to churn,
Master Jimmy," said she, watching his smiles
as she spoke.

"I ought to have got it out of the way by
half-past five, and all made into balls; but I
don't have a nice little boy like you come
visiting me every day, and I can't bear to
disappoint you."

"Thank you, Mrs. Chick," said Jimmy.

He supposed it would be nothing but fun to make butter, and secretly hoped he might be allowed to pat it into balls.

After breakfast he followed his kind hostess into the shed, and saw her pour a jar of rich cream into the green churn. She placed a chair for Jimmy beside the churn.

"All you've got to do," said she, "is to turn the handle of the churn 'round and 'round and 'round."

"Oh, that's nothing; I can do it just as easy," replied Jimmy.

Mrs. Chick laughed.

"It's harder than you think, little dear. But when you are tired of it you can let me know. I shall be close by in the kitchen, making pies." ‹

"Look here! see what I'm doing! You never churned any butter, now did you, Edy?"

"No," said Edith; "and I don't want to. "I'd rather help Mrs. Chick make pies."

For two minutes Jimmy was triumphant.

"How easy it goes! How well I do it!" he thought. "My arms must be pretty strong."

But nobody was there to hear or see him. Mrs. Chick had gone into the kitchen, and was talking to Edith about buttering the plates for the pies. Through the open shed door he espied the kid nibbling leaves from some low bushes. The little Morse baby, who never stayed at home if she could help it, had brought her black doll just inside Mrs. Chick's yard, and was rolling her in the sand.

"What a dirty baby to do that!" thought Jimmy.

Still he almost wished she would come into the shed; he did not enjoy being alone.

He turned the handle of the churn 'round and 'round and 'round. He was growing tired.

"Mrs. Chick!" he called out, "I think the butter is done."

But Mrs. Chick paid no attention. She was telling Edy how hard she used to work when she was a little girl named Biddy Roberts, and lived in England.

"Perhaps," said she to Edy, "they wouldn't have called me Biddy if they had known I was going to marry a man by the name of Chick!"

"Mrs. Chick!" called Jimmy again.

"Well, what is it, dear?" said she from the kitchen.

"The butter's done, I guess. Will you please come and see if the butter is done?"

Mrs. Chick was very busy. She had put some pie-crust on a deep plate, and was scalloping the crust into a kind of high wall all around the plate, ready to hold a rich custard.

"I think it's done; I do truly," repeated Jimmy.

"No, sonny; the butter can't have come yet. What are you doing? Don't take off the cover of the churn, Jimmy-boy. Only keep on turning the handle 'round and 'round and 'round."

"Why, that's just what I did do! Why, I've turned it 'round forty-two hundred times. I know I have. Can't I stop now and get a drink of water?"

Mrs. Chick laughed. She was a woman who laughed very easily.

"Yes; get some water if you like."

There was a large olla (oya) in one corner of the shed, covered by a white soup-plate. The water in it was always cold. Jimmy left the churn at once, and went to the olla, and stood to take a long breath. Then he ran to the pantry for a tumbler; he did not like to drink from the tin dipper which sat in the soup-plate.

But while he was gone for the tumbler, the

Morse baby slipped into the shed, making hardly any noise. She came in with that dirty, dirty doll, as full of sand as a pepper-box is full of pepper. She climbed into Jimmy's chair, lifted the cover off the churn, which was only set on edgewise, and said, " Diny, oo go in dare ! "

And then she plumped Dinah head-first into the churn.

Nobody heard or saw her. What made her do it ? It is of no use trying to guess. She might have thought such a sandy doll ought to have a bath. Or perhaps she was making believe Dinah had been naughty, and she was shutting her up in the closet.

At any rate, as soon as the miserable black object was safe in the churn, Baby Morse ran away to chase the kid, and forgot all about her doll.

When Jimmy had drunk two tumblers of water, and rested a long while, — for he was not in the least haste, — he went back to the churn.

The cover was off.

" I did not know I took that off," said he. And he put it on again quickly.

Then he turned the handle 'round and 'roound and 'ro-o-ound. But how ha-rd it went! Much harder than before. How heavy the cream had grown all at once ! Mrs. Chick had warned Jimmy that it would seem to grow very heavy at the last.

" Do come, Mrs. Chick!" he cried eagerly. " The butter's done now. I know it's done. It breaks my arm off to turn it 'round."

Mrs. Chick had just put her second pie into the oven. She went out to the shed, wondering what Jimmy meant, for she was sure the butter had not come. She took off the cover of the churn and looked in.

" Why! what's this ? " cried she.

She put in her hand then, and drew out that dirty, dirty doll.

She could not help laughing, though she
was very sorry.   It was quite too bad to spoil
so much cream, and she was by no means
a rich woman.

" I'm glad I didn't put in all my cream,"
she thought. " I had sense enough to save
out half of it."

But she was just as much amused as either
of the children.   She never was cross or sad,
whatever happened.

" Of course Baby Morse has been here,"
said she; " nobody else would cut up such a
caper. But I haven't seen her or heard a
sound of her all the morning."

" I saw her," said Jimmy. " She was play-
ing in the dirt with that horrid black thing;
but who'd ' a ' thought of her dropping it in
the churn ? "

Then they had another hearty laugh, all
three of them; and Jimmy never dreamed that
he had been at all to blame. The cream was

the color of Mrs. Chick's gray gown. She poured it into a pan, to save it for the animals, and then washed the churn.

" I won't scold the boy; it was all my own fault," thought she. " It's well I'm going to take these children home to-day. If they were to stay here much longer, I should let 'em pull the house down over my head. — Do you hear what I say, Biddy Chick ? "

Mrs. Dunlee was very much surprised that afternoon to see Edy walk into the house wrapped in an old shawl, of Mrs. Chick's, which almost tripped her up at every step.

" O mamma!" she cried, throwing up her arms, " my dress was just burnt off me ! The back of it, I mean."

And while Mrs. Chick was trying to tell the story, Edith began to laugh and cry wildly.

" O mamma!" said she, casting herself on her mother's neck, " you always did just right with me ; you knew best when you wouldn't trust me with candles and things. I *am* the careless-est girl ! "

" There! I'm glad you've found it out," retorted Kyzie. " You never believed it when anybody else said so."

Mamma raised a warning finger, and Kyzie was ashamed, and held her peace. She was the dearest girl in the world, but liked to lecture Edith ; and Mrs. Dunlee thought Edith did not need any lectures now. She was feeling very humble.

"O mamma!" she went on, "I should think you'd tie my feet and hands with a rope! yes, I should! Too bad I burnt up Mrs. Chick's pretty rug! But then, oh, dear! just think, you know, if there hadn't been any rug ! "

To divert their minds, Mrs. Chick told the story of Jimmy's butter. They were much amused ; but the funniest part of it was to hear her say, —

"But it was all my fault. I needn't have been so weak-minded."

When she left next morning there was a roll under the wagon-seat done up in brown paper. She had not known that the roll was there till she got home, when she found it contained a beautiful rug — a far better one than had been burned.

"Just like Mrs. Dunlee! She knew if I should see it before I came away I should hate to take it. And what's this? A bran new shawl! Well, well, well! She's a good woman, if there is one. Do you hear what I say, Biddy Chick?"

VII

THE BOY FROM NEW YORK

In October a little boy came from New York with his father to visit Major Irwin. It was Gilly's cousin, Dick Somers; and Dick was destined to get Jimmy into trouble.

He was a boastful boy. He told wonderful stories about the city of New York, where the houses went as high as Jack's beanstalk, and the people had so much money that they almost threw it away.

Dick had left a dog at home which seemed to him now as large as a small burro. Yes, he was sure of it. A dog much brighter than Punch Dunlee, as well as vastly handsomer.

Dick had a beautiful sister; there was no one like her in California. She had been

married six weeks before this in church ; and
" I tell you what, they spread carpets all over
the streets for Maggie to walk on ; yes, they
did ! "

Gilbert only laughed at these remarkable
tales ; but they annoyed Jamie, because they
made him feel so very inferior.

He tried in his turn to remember and relate
strange things that had happened to him or
that he had seen ; but he did not succeed
very well. Dick despised rattlesnakes, horned
toads, gophers, and road-runners. He would-
n't believe there are quicksands in California,
where you can "slump down, down, clear out
of sight."

" Pooh ! you needn't tell *me !* "

It was very discouraging to talk to Dick ;
still Jimmy was always ready to talk.

One Saturday morning, Dick and Gilbert
came over to the Dunlees' to play with Jimmy,
who was glad to see them. It was very still in

and about the house that morning. Mr. Sanford had been gone to the city of Washington
for many weeks, and it always seemed odd
without Mr. Sanford. To-day papa was visiting a sick man just out of town; Mrs. Porter,
over the way, had borrowed the baby; Kyzie
and Edith were having a botany lesson with
Aunt Vi somewhere in a canyon; and Lucy
had gone to Lincoln Heights to spend the day.

"What a merry time the little boys seem
to be having in the stable!" remarked Mrs.
Dunlee to Vendla, as they heard the sound
of childish laughter floating in on the air.

She had asked Jimmy to get some hens'
eggs; for she and Vendla were to make some
cake for tea by a new recipe. There was no
haste about the eggs, however. Vendla stood
by the pantry window rolling out pie-crust with
a glass rolling-pin, and would not be ready to
begin upon the cake till her four pies had gone
into the oven.

Ah, that cake which had not been baked yet, that cake by the new rule! If Mrs. Dunlee and Vendla had only known what strange thing would happen to it that after-noon they certainly would not have made it at all! But they did not know; and Mrs. Dunlee very soon took down a large baking-pan and buttered it, saying to herself all the while that she hoped the baby was behaving well at Mrs. Porter's. She missed him, and missed her three girls, and thought what a happy mother she was with five such dear children. Yet, after all, she was not sorry to have them out of the house for once on a Saturday morning.

"There's Jimmy laughing again, above the other boys. He's a noisy child; I wonder if Baby Eddy will be as fond of fun as Jimmy? Well, at any rate, I hope they'll both grow up to be good.

"'And if they fall, or if they rise,
Be each, pray God, a gentleman.'"

Now it was time for the cake.

"Jimmy, Jimmy!" called Mrs. Dunlee from the window. "You may bring the eggs now."

All this while the little boys in the stable had been chatting, and had hardly thought of the eggs.

"Billy Dow thrashed me last night," said Gilbert, shaking his fist at the rafters. "But I tell you I paid him off."

"Paid him off, that big fellow?" said Jimmy.

"Of course! Did you s'pose Gilly was going to forgive him?" cried the little cousin from New York contemptuously. "Would you forgive a boy that thrashed you, Jimmy Dunlee?"

"Ye-es, — if I couldn't catch him! If he was ever so much larger'n me!" was Jimmy's candid reply.

Gilly laughed. "*I* don't forgive 'em 'cause they're big! If I didn't dare hit Billy, I could call him awful names, and run out my tongue at him; couldn't I? Guess he won't try to thrash *me* again!"

"What did you call him?" asked Jimmy, much interested.

"'Billee! Billee!' says I, as loud as I could screech; 'Billee, you're an old monkey-wrench!' says I."

"Why!" exclaimed Jimmy, struck by Gilly's boldness. "Why-ee! I've had some o' those big boys call me a monkey; that's bad enough!"

"Yes; but I said monkey-wrench," said Gilly proudly.

"I was the one that told him the word!" cried Dick, eager to share in the praise; "it's a word they have in New York."

Not one of the three little boys thought of asking, "What is a monkey-wrench?" It sounded like something too bad to be talked about.

"What's that queer noise?" asked Dick.

It was John laughing all by himself in
the stall at what the boys were saying. But
when Jimmy peeped through the slats of the
stall at the pretty chocolate-and-white cow,
John stood there looking as solemn as an owl.

"We'll get our eggs first, and then go in
and play with Jessie," said Jimmy, thinking
this a great pleasure. But Dick, who had
hardly ever seen a cow, was secretly afraid
of Jessie's "hooks."

"Let's see which'll get the most eggs,"
said he, beginning to climb the ladder to the
mow.

And now began a hand-and-knee exploring-
expedition after eggs.

"Needn't dig so deep," said Jimmy, as Dick
thrust both arms up to the elbows in the
straw.

"Well, but I've found an egg, Jimmy Dunlee, and you haven't! Just as yellow! Do
you keep yellow hens?"

The laugh was now against Dick, who "didn't know everything," so Gilly said, "even if he did come from New York."

" I've found two eggs," said Gilly, "so, now, what you think ? "

" And I've found four," cried Jimmy, trying to pitch his voice on a subdued key. Too much triumph might be impolite to his guests.

" Why, here are two more, makes four. I found 'em myself," said Gilbert grandly. " What does your mamma do with so many eggs ? "

" She's going to put these in a cake."

" I like mince-pies better'n cake," returned Gilbert.

" I don't eat 'em," responded the boy from New York disdainfully, "and my mamma's fankful I don't ! "

" What *do* you eat ? " asked Jimmy.

Dick considered a moment.

" Apple-pie and cream candy and wedding-

cake. Sometimes I eat bread and butter — if
there's jelly on it."

"Oh!" said Jimmy with great respect, min-
gled perhaps with a little envy.

Did this come of living "back East" in
New York? What more delightful than to
be Dick Somers, and live where you have
wedding-cake every day of your life!

"But," ventured Jimmy with rising courage,
"maybe this will be wedding-cake that mamma's going to make. She didn't say."

The other boys laughed, and Dick said, —

"Pooh! I know better'n that! Say, none of
your sisters ever went and got married, did
they, Jim?"

Went and got married! His little sisters!
Jimmy pondered on this foolish question. Dick
meant it as an insult to his mamma's cooking,
no doubt, though he could not see how. Making sport of her cake, indeed, and before it
was baked!

Jimmy had tried to be polite to the boys as his guests ; but boys who go visiting ought to be polite too.

"Dick Somers!" cried Jimmy in a towering rage, "you stop that! I don't care if you did come from New York, you don't know any more about my mamma's cake than you do about — about horned toads, so there!"

It was just here that the pleasant voice called from the pantry window, —

"Jimmy, Jimmy, you may bring the eggs now."

It was well that something should cut short Jimmy's angry speech. It was not safe to discuss horned toads above all things with Dick. Jimmy always grew furious to hear Dick talk so wisely about them, when, as Gilly said, "he wouldn't know one from a caterpillar;" whereas Jimmy had raised a whole family of the queer little creatures, and knew them like A B C.

VIII

THE MISSING CAKE

IT was pretty warm that Saturday afternoon, but a strong southerly breeze was blowing. Vendla had just set the last clean dishes on the pantry shelf, and gone up-stairs, when her mistress heard the sound of something falling, and, going into the pantry, found that the screen had fallen out of the window. Jimmy stood just outside, talking with John, and the screen had fallen close to Jimmy's feet.

" Here, little one," said John, " if you'll hand that up to me, I'll pound it in so it won't come out. But what made you ask about quicksands ? "

" Oh, to tell Dick Somers ! He won't believe a word I say."

" That's the little fellow from New York,
is it ? Well, you tell him it's all true. He
can sink up to his ears in a quicksand, and
he may try it if he wants to."

" There! there! I knew it all the time,"
cried Jimmy. "I wish you'd tell him I did
see two live rattlesnakes, and I did see — oh,
lots of road-runners! He thinks I'm a pretty
nearly fool! Almost ! "

Mrs. Dunlee heard this scrap of conversation as Jimmy was entering the house. He
came along to the pantry, looking rather vexed
and discontented. His mother suspected he
was thinking of the New York boy, and wondered a little that he should be so anxious
to go that very afternoon to return his visit.
Dick did not seem to be a very agreeable
companion, yet he had a sort of fascination
for Jimmy.

Jimmy-boy lingered about the pantry. The
frosted cake " made by a new rule " sat cooling

on a platter, and the flies outside on the win-
dow-screen were wildly longing to get in and
have a share; but the wire they beat against
was hard and strong, and would not let them
in.

Jimmy did not blame the flies for desiring
the cake. It was certainly beautiful to be-
hold. Could Dick Somers ever have seen anything more spotlessly fair, even in the great
city of New York?

" Mamma, is this a wedding-cake ? "

" No, dear ; we only have wedding-cake when
people are married."

" Oh, I forgot that ! 'Course we don't ! "

Jimmy looked abashed. How could he have
been so stupid ? He knew now why the boys
had laughed at him. Yes, and why Dick Somers was always enjoying such an astonishing
amount of wedding-cake. Dick's sister had
been married in church, and the whole city
had been carpeted for her to walk on, or so

Dick pretended. And naturally there had been bushels and bushels of cake.

" When are you going to cut this, mamma ? "

" To-night, my son."

" Oh, goody ! Wish I had a piece this minute to carry to the boys ! Dick Somers thinks we don't have anything good out here. Why, mamma, he just makes fun of everything in California ! "

" You may give him a piece to-morrow, Jamie."

" May I ? "

The little boy gazed wistfully at the cake. He knew mamma had frosted it on purpose to please her children ; she and papa never ate any frosting.

" It does look so smooth and nice before it is cut up. If Dick could only see it all whole ! "

Jimmy seemed to be talking to himself, rather than to his mother, and Mrs. Dunlee did not answer him. But she recalled the remark afterwards, indeed that very evening, after something had happened of which I am about to tell you.

"I must go up-stairs now to change my dress," said she.

Jimmy followed her out of the pantry, and she shut the door.

"Where are you going, my son?" asked papa a little later, coming home from his ride, and meeting Jimmy running off at full speed.

"To Gilly Irwin's, papa; mamma said I might."

Jimmy was in a hurry, — Mr. Dunlee observed it, — in an unusual hurry. And, as he rushed away like a whirlwind, he paused an instant to pick up a basket which stood under the large pepper-tree.

"I wonder what scheme the boy has in hand now," said Mr. Dunlee to himself. "There's not a man in town who carries on so much business as our James."

Mrs. Dunlee came down-stairs fresh and smiling in her new cambric dress with lace trimmings, and sat with her husband in the shaded study. While she sewed, he read aloud, or sometimes he dropped his book, and they had a little chat.

It seemed very still, they both said. Not a sound, even of Vendla stepping about the kitchen, for Vendla was up-stairs sewing.

" How we do miss the children ! " said Mrs. Dunlee.

And they agreed that they missed the " Prince Imperial," as they called the baby, more than any one of the others. He was such a rollicking prince, never speaking a single word, but ruling his loving subjects by laughter and tears, and sometimes by a wave of his royal hand.

At four o'clock he was brought home in

Mrs. Porter's arms, beaming with joy ; but refused to tell where he had been, or who had given him the string of pretty shells he wore on his neck. He only smiled and cooed, and mamma knelt at his feet, and said he was " the sweetest baby ever was born."

Then Lucy came home with two of her cousins. She had visited a photographer with Aunt Jessie, and a man had "tooken her picture."

" He kissed his hand to me, papa, and then he tooked it. But I don't know where it is now."

" Did you keep still, little daughter ? "

" Oh, yes, papa ; I kept just as still ! I was very *gemplumly.*"

It had long been Lucy's ambition to be "gemplumly, just like Jimmy."

In a few minutes the two older girls came home. They brought a box full of wildflowers, and were rather flushed and tired and

talkative. Very hungry too ; for a " tramp
dog" had eaten most of their luncheon. Edy
was afraid if she didn't have something to
eat in one minute, her head would fly into
pieces, it ached so hard.

"We can't allow that," said mamma. "Go
into the dining-room, every one of you ! Draw
up your chairs to the table, and I'll bring you
a plate of bread and butter."

She went with a light step into the pantry ;
but when she returned there was a cloud on
her face.

" I don't know what to think," said she, setting a plate of bread and the butter-dish on the
table. " I baked a loaf of cake this morning,
intending it for tea ; but it is gone ! Vendla !"
she called, going to the back staircase.

Vendla came down, looking rather serious.

" I went into the pantry half an hour ago,
ma'am," said she, "and there was the empty
platter sitting on the shelf. And, thinks I,

'Where's that cake? Mrs. Dunlee must have put it in the cake-chest.' But I looked in the chest, and it wasn't there. And that's all I know about it."

"Why didn't you come at once and tell me, Vendla?"

The girl hesitated.

"I thought you might feel troubled about it, ma'am. I was afraid you'd think "—

Mrs. Dunlee knew she would have said, "I was afraid you'd think Master Jimmy took it."

But Vendla could not speak the words, and Mrs. Dunlee liked her all the better for it.

"My good girl," said she, "did you go downstairs and lock the back door this afternoon when I asked you to do so."

"Yes, ma'am."

"And you saw no one about the house at that time, Vendla?"

"No, ma'am. Master Jimmy had just gone out. I heard his papa ask, 'Where are you going?' And Master Jimmy answered, 'To Gilly Irwin's.' That was just as I stood locking the back door. And after that Mr. Dunlee came into the front hall, and I heard him hasp the screen door. I'm sure I did, ma'am."

"And then you went up-stairs again, Vendla? And you didn't go into the pantry?"

'No, ma'am; I went straight up-stairs. I was in a hurry to finish my blouse waist."

"And you heard no one going or coming?"

"No, ma'am. Only once I heard John's step; he was looking after the cow."

' "That will do, Vendla; I don't know what to think about this!"

As Vendla left the dining-room, Kyzie looked up quickly, exclaiming, "O mamma, don't look so! I can't believe it was Jimmy!"

"Neither can I," said Aunt Vi, forgetting to eat her bread and butter.

"It doesn't seem in the least like him," returned Mrs. Dunlee.

But she had grown quite pale, and was going toward the study when her husband
entered the dining-room. He had overheard
part of the conversation, and looked as amazed
and distressed as his wife.

"Why, my dear," said he, "it is incredible!"

"So it is, James. The boy is too old to do
such a thing; he has too much conscience.
But the question is, who took the cake?
It could not have gone without hands."

"I see, I see, Prudy. And the doors were
all well fastened, and you and I sitting there
in the study."

"And the house so still," added Mrs. Dunlee. "You know we spoke two or three times
of the stillness."

Mr. Dunlee paced the floor in deep thought.

"There must be a way out of this," he
said.

"The cat, you know," suggested Edith.

"Yes," said Aunt Vi; "there's always a cat

to be suspected when there has been mis-chief."

" I'm afraid he put it in his basket," went on Mrs. Dunlee, referring of course to Jimmy, and not the cat.

" He said he wanted some of the cake for those boys, Gilly Irwin and his cousin; and I told him he might have a piece to-morrow. But he didn't seem quite satisfied ; I remember it now distinctly. He said, ' It does look so smooth and nice before it is cut up. If Dick could only see it all whole!' "

" What reply did you make ? " asked Mr. Dunlee.

" I believe I didn't make any reply. Do you suppose, now, Jimmy could have thought I meant to give him the cake ? "

" Hardly likely," said Mr. Dunlee. " But there is one possibility I can think of. He may have taken it to show to the boys, in-tending to bring it back uncut and uninjured.

I know he had a basket in his hand; that large one he carries."

" Did he really have that basket ? " returned Mrs. Dunlee. " Then it does look very much as if he put the cake in it ! Hush ! isn't that Jimmy's step in the hall ? "

IX

THE INDIAN BASKET

JIMMY–BOY came in swinging his basket on his arm. It was a remarkably pretty Indian basket ; and ever since Aunt Vi had given it to him two weeks ago, it had travelled with him wherever he went.

"Jimmy," said his mother as the little feet reached the threshold, " Jimmy, I would like to see you in the study."

The tone was grave ; the boy looked up in alarm. Mamma was sure to be "in earnest" when she spoke like this, and wished to see him in the study.

The moment they entered the study she closed the door and turned and looked at him. What was she going to say ?

" Jamie, O Jamie! did you carry it off in the basket ? "

" Carry what off, mamma ? "

" He speaks very innocently, as if it were quite new to him," thought his mother.

She took the basket from his hand, and measured it with her eye. Yes, it was large enough; it could easily have held the whole loaf. But it was empty now. If Jimmy had carried off the loaf to show to the boys, he had not brought it back.

" My son, where is the cake I baked and frosted this morning ? "

" I don't know ! Why, mamma, you didn't s'pose *I* took that cake ? "

There was a quiver of pain in the young voice. Mrs. Dunlee looked at her child eagerly, as if she would read his very soul.

" Did you take it, Jamie ? You said you wanted to show it to Dick Somers; you wished him to see it before it was cut. Now the cake is gone. Did you take it ? "

The tone was very gentle, but it moved
Jimmy strangely. He hung his head and
burst into tears. Was he sorry he had been
found out? Or did it grieve him to be suspected wrongfully?

"No, mamma," said he; "I never did it."

"Jimmy, I want the truth! Remember your
dear Heavenly Father hears what you say."

Jimmy only sobbed the harder at this.

"If you took the cake, and are sorry for
it, I will forgive you."

"O mamma! did you think I took it?"

"I hope not, my dear. Only we don't know
what has become of it. And you said you
wanted Dick Somers to see that we have nice
things in California."

Jimmy writhed in strong excitement.

"Yes, mamma, he's just the meanest boy!
I wish I could tell you how mean he is.
When I carried him the" —

Jimmy paused suddenly. There was silence

for half a minute while he struggled with himself. It seemed as if he were almost on the
point of confession, and something held him
back. Was it so? His mother could not
be sure, for he would not let her see his
face.

"So you carried something to Dick? What
was it, Jamie?"

"O mamma, mamma! don't ask me. I can't
tell. He was so mean about it, mamma!"

About the cake? Mrs. Dunlee wondered.
Had Dick teased the little boy by finding
fault with it? If so, Jimmy would not like
to tell her. A word against his mother,
or against anything his mother did, was always very hard for Jimmy to bear.

"What did Dick say or do that was mean,
my son? Do not be afraid to tell mamma."

"Oh, I can't tell you what he said!"

Jimmy had not looked up at all, and now
he hid his face in his hands.

"If he was innocent, why should he do so? Why shouldn't he look at me?" thought Mrs. Dunlee, her heart aching with grief and pity.

But it was useless urging him. At any allusion to the cake he exclaimed, —

"No, mamma, I never."

As if, having once said the words, he was determined to go on repeating them over and over. There had always been a strain of obstinacy in Jimmy's character, as his mother was well aware. She turned sorrowfully away, and left the little boy alone in the study, his face buried deep in his father's easy-chair.

It was a sad evening for everybody. Even the Prince Imperial ceased to enjoy his string of shells, and became too low-spirited to smile. No one but Kyzie had much hope of Jimmy's innocence; but Kyzie said, —

"It wasn't one bit like Jimmy-boy to take the cake in the first place. And then he never would lie about it! Mamma, do think again; couldn't a thief have slipped into the house ever so softly by the back door?

"It only makes you sigh, mamma; you think it's so absurd. I know it's absurd. Somebody took that cake off the shelf, and left the platter, and it seems as if it must be Jimmy. Still, I can't believe 'twas Jimmy. I almost think 'twas somebody that dropped down through the 'sky-hole.'"

She meant the window in the roof. Lucy called it the sky-hole.

Mr. Dunlee turned as he was pacing the floor.

"I am almost as unreasonable as Katharine," said he; "I can't give it up that Jamie is guilty. I must have a little talk with him myself before I am convinced."

He went into the study. The poor boy was still crying bitterly. Mr. Dunlee seated himself in the big chair, and took him in his arms.

"Perhaps you thought mamma meant to give you the cake? Was that what you thought? To divide with your little friends?"

Jimmy could not answer.

"If so, that was only a mistake. Perhaps you carried it away, and cut it up in big pieces for the boys? Tell papa all about it."

"O papa! I can't tell; but I never touched the cake."

"Then what did you carry off in your basket?"

"O papa! please don't ask me," wailed Jimmy. "'Twas something — something I can't talk about! I promised not to."

"My son, this grows more and more mysterious. I can't urge you to break a promise, though why you should have made one I can't possibly see. If you promised not to tell about the cake, that was wrong, and " —

Jamie raised his head earnestly. "O papa! don't you believe me when I speak?"

"My precious child, I do so long to believe you!"

Jimmy slipped down from his father's knee,
and stood upright before him, his eyes shining
with a new thought.

" Does God know everything, papa?"

"Certainly, my child."

" Well, then, when you go to heaven, papa,
you just ask God if I haven't told you the
truth," said Jimmy; and broke down again,
and shook with sobs.

Mr. Dunlee caught the little pleader in his
arms. He knew no more than before what
had become of the cake, but he was sure from
that moment that Jimmy had not taken it.

" If he had, he never would have dared
make a speech like that," said the minister to
his wife as he came out of the study, looking much happier than when he had gone
in.

"I hope you are right; I believe you are

"Jamie, O, Jamie, did you carry it off?"

Page 114.

right," replied Mrs. Dunlee, her eyes brimming with tears. "Still, we must wait a while to make sure."

The next day, Sunday, was not a happy one. The older children knew the exceeding sinfulness of a lie, and it was certain that Jimmy knew it also. Yet what had become of the cake ?

" Jimmy, what's the matter o' you ? " asked wee Lucy, going up to her brother, and putting her little arms around his neck.

"Oh, they just despise me as hard as anything ! " he replied.

It broke his heart to be "despised." He did not know how everybody pitied and longed to help him, or he would not have been so unhappy.

Just before dinner Kyzie happened to go into the pantry. As she was returning to the kitchen she heard a noise at the pantry window, like the rattling of dishes, and, looking that way, saw Jessie, the pretty cow, eating a custard-pie.

The pie was sitting on the window-ledge, within easy reach, and Jessie was helping herself without fork or spoon.

" Come, mamma! come quick!" cried Kyzie.

Mamma came; and Jessie stood still, and finished the pie before her eyes, licking the plate too, as though she would not miss a morsel.

" Did you ever see such impudence?" said Kyzie, laughing.

But mamma was not listening.

" Jessie ate that cake!" she exclaimed. " Where is John?"

John was surprised to see every one so excited.

" I let the cow out into the back yard yesterday about two minutes," said he; "but I never thought of her cutting up a caper in the pantry! When I went after her, she was standing close to the pantry window, to be sure, and the screen was out. I put it back; and thinks I, 'That's the second time I've done it to-day. I'll fix that screen Monday so it will act ·better.' "

" Did you see Jessie eating the cake ? "

" No, ma'am ; she must have swallowed it pretty spry, for I never saw a crumb of ˙it."

" O Jessie, Jessie ! we never knew you were a thief ! " said Edith, hugging the pretty animal whose " sweet tooth " had caused all this trouble.

Mrs. Dunlee had no time or thought for the cow. She was watching the happy smiles on Jimmy's face.

" My precious, innocent boy ! " said she, holding him close, as if she could never let him go.

" You made a mistake when you said the cake couldn't have gone without hands ; didn't

you, mamma?" said Kyzie, trying to laugh;
but somehow the tears would come first.

"Mamma," whispered Jimmy-boy, — and a
lighter-hearted boy you never saw, — "mamma,
put your ear down close; I want to say something. I knew all the time I didn't do it, and
I knew God knew I didn't do it."

"Yes, dear; that is so."

"And I knew God would tell you and
papa all about it when you got to heaven,
mamma; but, oh, I didn't want to wait!"

"No, you dear, suffering child," replied his
mother. "And, thank God, we didn't any of
us have to wait! We're so glad to know it
all now!"

And then she kissed Jimmy on his mouth
and hair and eyes; and the children all gath-
ered around, and Kyzie said, —

"Isn't this a beautiful Sunday? I'd rather
have it than a diamond ring."

It was not till Tuesday that they learned

what Jimmy had carried off in the basket; and then Mr. Somers, Dick's father, told it, laughing, to Mr. Dunlee. It was horned toads.

Little Dick had declared that they had eyes in the backs of their heads. Jimmy and Gilbert disputed this, and told him to look for himself.

"I won't look," said Dick. "Guess I *know!* I'll leave it to my *papa* if I don't know!"

The more he was laughed at, the more he insisted, saying at last, —

"I'll give you five cents, Jimmy Dunlee, for every toad you'll find that *hasn't* got eyes back of his head! Bring 'em along, sir, and let my papa see 'em, and I'll give you fi—ive cents apiece!"

So Jimmy, expecting to make a small fortune, had roamed far and wide, and collected five toads; for he could not spare his

tame ones. But when he took them to
Major Irwin's, Dick only said, —

"What you s'pose *I* want o' those toads?"
Jimmy was angry.

"You *told* me to bring 'em! Look at 'em
now; look this minute! You *said* they had
eyes back o' their heads!"

Dick was laughed at by the whole family,
and made to confess that these were the
first horned toads he had ever seen. His
father called him "a little braggart;" and
for once in his life the boy was ashamed,
and ran crying down cellar to hide.

Jimmy threw back his shoulders proudly.
It was a great triumph to have humbled
Dick Somers! And then, besides that, to
have earned twenty-five cents!

But when he modestly asked for his
money, what did those people all do but fall
to laughing again?

And the wider his honest brown eyes

opened with surprise, the harder they all laughed!

Jimmy could not see anything funny in the affair; he only saw that he had been cheated and imposed upon. As he turned indignantly on his heel, Hatty Irwin, Gilbert's sister, said in a low tone, —

"The little toad-merchant is going home to see if his mamma will buy his toads."

Hatty did not expect to be overheard; but Jimmy caught the words, and was cut to the heart. He shouted wildly, —

"I shall *not* tell my mamma! I shall *not* tell any single body at my house, so there!"

And all the while he was running away from these cruel people as fast as he could go.

If he had not made this sudden, impulsive promise to Hatty, all might have been different. For then he would have related his woes to his own family; mamma would have pitied and soothed him; and, better than all, there would have been no mystery as to what was carried off in the basket.

Instead of that, — but you know the story, and can fancy how poor Jimmy-boy suffered.

Dick Somers went home that very week; and Mrs. Dunlee said to her husband, —

"I am really glad for Jimmy's sake. I am sure Jimmy has not been made very happy by the little boy from New York."

X

A GREAT SECRET

PEOPLE were beginning to think and talk about Christmas. There was a pleasant stir in the air of something mysterious and delightful about to happen. Mamma and Aunt Vi were often together in Aunt Vi's "snuggery" up-stairs, and what they were consulting about nobody ventured to ask; some uncommonly fine present for each of the children, no doubt.

One day Aunt Vi, who was sewing in the back parlor, looked up from her work, and said, —

"Jimmy-boy, do you think you could go to the store and buy me some blue sewing-silk like this pattern?"

And she held up a bit of blue satin.

"Why don't you ask *me*, Auntie?" exclaimed Edith, dropping the doll she was dressing in a new tea-gown. "Boys don't know the difference between a skein of silk and a clothes-line."

Aunt Vi secretly thought that she could trust Jimmy better than Edith, but she did not like to say so.

"Then you may get me the silk, if you will, Edith; two spools."

"Well, I'll go with you," said Jimmy-boy.

"If you're going, I'll have to go too," piped wee Lucy.

"Of course," thought Edith. "And there's the dog, *he'll* have to follow, — the 'inevitable dog,' Aunt Vi calls him. Oh, dear!"

"If the whole family is to go, we may as well have more errands done!" exclaimed mamma with a playful smile. "Can I trust you, Edith, to call at our grocer's, Mr. Ladd's,

and ask him to send me two pounds of Santa
Isabel butter?"

"'Can I trust you?'" repeated Edith to herself. "Why do people always say that to me,
as if they didn't feel *sure?*"

"Yes, mamma," she added aloud; "two
pounds blue silk, two spools San Isabel's
butter;" then corrected her own mistake,
laughing.

The little party went skipping along in a
very gay mood, the "inevitable dog" at their
heels. Instead of proceeding at once to the
stores, Edith chose to go two or three blocks
out of the way, to watch a couple of tiny
boys riding together on the back of a burro,
and·to see how fast the workmen were get-
ting on in building a tall house she greatly
admired.

They passed Mrs. Phillips's brown cottage,
with the bird-of-paradise flowers in the garden. Edith had a fancy for these gay, grace-

ful flowers, with their very long scarlet
streamers floating on the air like little ban-
ners. But just now she should not have
gone that way; it was one of her mistakes.
Her mother had said to her only the day
before, —

"Edith, when you are out with Lucy, I would
prefer you shouldn't go near Mrs. Phillips's
house, for I don't like to expose Lucy to
whooping-cough."

Edith would not have "exposed" her little
sister on any account if she had only stopped
to think. She believed whooping-cough to be almost sure death. Hadn't she had it herself just
before Jimmy was born, and nearly died of it?
So she firmly believed. At any rate, the
nurse, Mrs. Chick, had not allowed her to
go near the new baby, — only think of that!
She had had to look at Jimmy through the
window! She was only two years old at the
time, and could not remember anything about

it, but this was what everybody said. It had always impressed Edith as something very strange and dreadful, that she had been shut away like that from her own baby Jimmy! And, after all, he had had whooping-cough just the same.

"Why, there's Sadie Phillips at the window!" said Jimmy. "What makes her face so red?"

Then all in a moment Edith stopped short in the street, and recalled her mother's warning. She had done the wickedest, dreadfullest thing in the world to take Lucy near that cottage! And alas, alas! Sadie Phillips was coughing; that was what made her face look so red. The window was closed, it is true; but Edith heard the frightful sound, and it fell on her heart like a knell.

"What made me come here? What shall I do?" she wailed, seizing her little sister in her arms, and running furiously down the street.

Wee Lucy screamed, the dog barked, and Jimmy cried out, "What is it? What is it?" not knowing what to make of this strange behavior.

" Oh, I've *esposed* Lucy! I've esposed Lucy!" cried wretched Edith, the tears raining down her cheeks.

Lucy struggled out of her arms, laughing. She did not know what "esposed" meant; neither did Jimmy; and it may be that Edith did not clearly know herself.

"O Lucy darling, don't laugh; it's dreadful; it's awful! What does make you act so, Jimmy? We must run, run, run! Lucy's going to have whooping-cough, sure as you live."

Upon that the small sister very naturally felt a tickling in the windpipe, and rasped her throat, trying to see if a cough would come. Nothing could have increased Edith's fright.

The better Lucy succeeded in coughing, the harder Edith cried, and the louder barked the wondering dog.

This delighted roguish Lucy. She liked to have Edith cry over her; it made her feel very important. She wished Jimmy would cry too ; but he only said coolly, —

"Hush, Lucy; you haven't got it ; you needn't *pertend*."

"I know she hasn't got it yet," replied Edith; "it takes a long while. But what I'm crying about is, she's going to get it! She's swallowed some ; she swallowed it when we stood by Sadie's house."

It was of no use for Jimmy to say "Pooh!" This was a matter of life and death to Edith. She wanted to take Lucy home at once, and perhaps have her shut in a dark room, or at any rate put to bed.

But those errands !

"Jimmy," said she, as they came in sight

of the stores, "my eyes don't look *very* red, do they?"

Truthful James had to reply, —

"Yes, they do, — red as a lobster cactus."

"Well, I can't help it. You stay out here with Punch and Lucy, while I go in for the silk."

"See here! I've thought of something," said Jimmy, touched by Edith's distress. "If Lucy did swallow some, can't they give her something to cure it? Mamma could, I guess, or Dr. Devoll."

"Why, I never thought of that," returned Edith, gathering courage.

"Now, Lucy, you *will* be willing to take a pill when we get home if mamma thinks it's best?"

Lucy wasn't quite sure. She thought it would depend somewhat upon the size of the pill, also upon the sort of jelly it was offered in.

"Oh, how she does act sometimes!" sighed Edith. "Now, Lucy, you stay out here with the dog and Jimmy; you stay out here till come back."

Lucy consented.

It was a red-eyed, broken-hearted little girl who entered Mr. Hall's store and asked for blue sewing-silk. You would hardly have known her for happy Edith Dunlee.

"Oh, no, sir," she said when a spool was offered her. "Not silk; *thread*. She wants to *sew* it!" The salesman looked surprised, then amused, then sorry; for by this time Edith had begun to cry again.

"Wouldn't it be well, little miss, for you to go home now, and come back again when you know your errand."

Edith had to confess that it would.

She went next to the grocer's for butter.

"I will send it up," said the clerk.

But no, Edith was sure mamma had intended that she should carry it.

It was given her in a paper bag, and she held the bag close to her heart, and cried over it ; and by the time they reached home the butter was ready to melt. She dropped it in a chair, and shrieked out, —

"O mamma, Lucy's been there ! I took her ! I *s'posed* her ! "

And down Edith sank upon the sofa in unspeakable woe. Little Lucy finished the direful story.

"Hookin'-cock, mamma, hookin'-cock ! Give me a pill ! Please put it in squinch jelly ! "

I must confess that mamma and Aunt Vi fell to laughing in the most unfeeling manner. Each tried in turn to soothe poor Edith ; and mamma said that even if Mrs. Phillips's window had been wide open, — and Jimmy was sure it was shut, — that even with the window open it was hardly probable that Lucy had been exposed in so short a time.

"And whooping-cough is nothing very serious nere in California, my daughter. Children suffer very little from it in this mild climate. I wouldn't mind Lucy's having it some time, say next spring; but just now," —

Here she looked at Aunt Vi, who blushed and smiled.

" It *would* be rather awkward just now," said Aunt Vi.

" Yes," returned Mrs. Dunlee ; "we mustn't have any whooping-cough in the house till after the wedding."

" Wedding?" repeated Edith, " what wedding ? "

" Am I not a stupid woman ! " exclaimed mamma, putting her hand over her mouth. " I came very near letting out a great secret."

" But is there going to be a wedding, mamma ? "

Edith's tears were dried now. She had thrown to the winds all her whooping-cough fright.

"Is there going to be a wedding, mamma?"

"Yes, dear, sometime and somewhere we hope there will be a wedding. It isn't quite time yet to talk much about it. Very soon you will know."

Edith looked from her mother to her aunt, her eyes full of questions. But before she had time to put the questions into words, Aunt Vi inquired about her blue sewing-silk. Too bad to have to stop and explain all that; for afterwards Edith couldn't find out the least thing about the wedding, — whose it was, or where or when. Papa pretended that it was very likely some Indians from Arizona.

"O papa! now you know it's not Indians! And it's nobody in Arizona either. The wedding belongs right here in California."

"Indeed! And possibly in this very house. Who knows?"

Edith felt that she was being trifled with.

Who was there in this house to be married but papa and mamma?

And they had been married already.

Then one day somebody said Mr. Henry Sanford was coming home from Washington.

"Oh, now I know!" cried Edith. "It's Mr. Sanford and Aunt Vi; it's Mr. Sanford and Aunt Vi!"

She was right. They were to be married at Christmas, just two weeks ahead.

"If Lucy doesn't have whooping-cough, you mean?" said Edith. "If she does, I s'pose you'll have to put off the wedding?"

No one answered this question. No one knew how it weighed upon Edith and Jimmy, or how closely they watched their little sister, fearing she might suddenly fall to coughing, and put a stop to the whole delightful and extraordinary plans for Christmas.

But Lucy did not cough, — except when somebody reminded her.

XI

A WEE WEDDING

CHRISTMAS was almost here. One morning Mrs. Dunlee went about the house singing, —

"The shepherds heard it overhead ;
    The joyful angels raised it then ;
'Glory to God on high !' it said,
'And peace on earth to gentle *men*.'"

"That's *me*," thought Jimmy. He felt that he had a private and particular claim on Christmas, for it was his birthday. Now birthdays were becoming an old story to Jimmy. He had had quantities of them, and this would be the sixth ; but a wedding was something new. "*What was a wedding ?*"

Sometimes people came to the house to be

married, and papa married them in the parlor, the children not being allowed to go in.
But that " didn't count ;" what was a *wedding ?*

" Where'll they put it ? " asked wee Lucy.

" It isn't a thing you can put anywhere ; it
isn't a vase or a teapot," replied Edith. " It's
only something that folks *do*. Aunt Vi is
going to marry Mr. Sanford, — no, he's going
to marry Aunt Vi."

This did not help the matter much.

" What do they do it for ? " asked Jimmy.

Edith herself was perplexed as to that, though
she did not like to own it.

" Oh, mamma says Mr. Sanford is coming
here because papa is a *minister!*" She spoke
proudly, as if the world held but one. " Papa
is a minister, and can do it just right. 'Twill
be a great deal worse than Thanksgiving and
Christmas. A monstrous cake, black as a
shoe, — Kyzie didn't mean I should know about

that, — and chicken salad, and lobster salad,
and I *think* turkey salad. Ice-cream, I know;
ice-cream, — ever so many colors, just like a
bed of flowers. And — and — well, I can't remember the rest."

Jimmy's eyes grew very brilliant. The
mention of black cake, and cream all the
colors of the rainbow, had placed the wedding
in a much clearer light. He went and re-
ported to wee Lucy, and Lucy mounted a
chair and told the looking-glass.

" Auntie's going to be mallied! Papa'll be
there in his pulpit right in the parlor. Roses
and i-scream ; worse'n Kismus, worse'n birf-
days ! "

" Cheer, boys, cheer ! " added Jimmy, by way
of chorus.

The night but one before the wedding he
and Lucy were strangely wide awake. Lucy
lay in her crib at least five minutes with open
eyes, wondering why *she* couldn't be married

as well as Aunt Vi. She meant to ask
mamma. When Jamie fell asleep it was to
dream of weddings. The weddings seemed
to be made chiefly of white and pink sugar,
and danced a ring-round-rosy with papa in
the middle, papa taking up a deal of room
on account of his pulpit.

There was one thing very remarkable indeed which Edith had not told Jimmy, simply
because she did not know it herself. He
learned it next day from dear Aunt Vi. It
was this : —

Jimmy was to be groomsman at the wedding, and Lucy was to be bridesmaid ! Somebody had been making a beautiful white frock
for little Lucy, all embroidered with silk apple-
blossoms. Some one else had been making
a charming blue suit for Jimmy, all spangled
with silver.

Why shouldn't these two children go nearly
wild with rapture ? Why shouldn't they think

the wedding was made on purpose for themselves, and that Aunt Vi had little to do with
it, except to look on and admire their new
clothes ?

Auntie had lived in the house ever since
they could remember. They loved her dearly,
and it was very sad that Mr. Sanford should
have taken this sudden notion to come and
carry her off to Washington.

"She'll never, never see any more cherry-
trees," thought Lucy. "Georgie has cut 'em
all down ! "

But they had little time to grieve over los-
ing their aunt, little time to pity her for
being obliged to go away ; their new clothes
filled all their thoughts. Jimmy felt that life
had nothing grander to offer him than the
honor of being " best man " at a wedding.
It was as if he was about to become a king,
and wear a royal crown.

As for Lucy, she was in such a flutter of

delight, that Kyzie had to watch her, lest she should run all over town to say to people, — "What you fink? I'se going to be mallied to Aunt Vi."

Mr. Sanford arrived from Washington the very day before Christmas. Lucky for him that he was in season for the wedding!

"May I tell him about it, mamma?" asked Lucy.

Mamma thought it would do no harm.

"There's going to be *sumfin'* at my house to-morrow, Mr. Sanford, worse'n *you* ever saw! And Jimmy and I are going to stand up in it. It's a wedding! *Wasn't* you glad you came?"

"Very glad! I wouldn't have missed it for anything. A wedding, do you say, Miss Snippet? Pray, who is the bride?"

And he looked solemnly at Aunt Vi, whose cheeks were the color of the buds on Lucy's rosebush.

Lucy could not answer. She did not 'member that she had heard anyfing about a bride.

Jimmy, who was kneeling before Mr. Sanford, had never heard of a bride.

" I'm groomsman, you know," said he, hoping he did not look as proud as he felt. " I'm groomsman, and Lucy is bridesmaid. We've got some *splendid* clothes ! But I don't believe there'll be any bride. Mamma never said anything about that."

"Ah! But, Jimmy, if I were you I would look around sharply, and try to find a bride. Brides are all the fashion nowadays at weddings."

" Oh ! " said Jimmy coldly. He never troubled his head about fashions. It struck him, too, that the Dunlees ought to be able to manage their own wedding, without the help of Mr. Sanford, a man who did not belong in the family. Still, being a boy of good manners, Jimmy refrained from speaking all his thoughts; he merely said, "Oh!"

Christmas dawned at last, birthday, wedding, and all. The house was full of presents; not for the children, though. *They* had very few this year. And in the evening people began to call. Whether the presents and the people made any part of the wedding Jimmy and Lucy could not fairly make out. Nothing more was heard of a bride.

The children had been dressed quite early, and afterwards kept up-stairs so long that they began to grow tired. By and by somebody gave each of them a very large bouquet and said, "Come."

They heard music, and, keeping step to it, marched gayly down-stairs. The parlor was full of people, all richly dressed, but none of them so fine as the little groomsman and bridesmaid — oh, by no means! — or half so well pleased with their clothes! Aunt Vi

and Mr. Sanford were going into the parlor
too.

Nobody spoke; that sweet music was play-
ing. Mamma whispered to Jimmy to take
Lucy's hand; and the two children went up
to join Aunt Vi and Mr. Sanford in the
bay-window. Lucy stood beside Aunt Vi, and
Jimmy-boy beside Mr. Sanford, as had been
agreed upon beforehand.

All heads were turned that way. The
little groomsman and bridesmaid felt that the
proud moment had come when they were to
be seen and admired by the whole world.
Lucy felt Aunt Vi tremble, and wondered
why she should be so frightened. Or was
she only cold? Lucy stole a quick glance at
her face. Why, how pale it looked! the pretty
pink color all gone out of her cheeks! Her
dress was soft, ·cream-colored silk, with only
lace on it, not half so sweet as the apple-
blossoms on Lucy's.

"The little groomsman and bridesmaid."

Page 150.

Lucy did not speak. She had promised
she wouldn't ; and besides, there was no
chance for anybody to speak. Papa was
standing there, just going to preach, though,
to be sure, he had no pulpit. It wasn't
much of a sermon, either. He only asked
some questions, and Aunt Vi and Mr. Sanford answered so low you could hardly hear.
Then there was a ring put on Aunt Vi's
finger, and papa talked some more, and prayed
a little.

Lucy drew a long breath, but kept per-
fectly quiet. Jimmy was quiet too, though
they both looked sober and surprised. *This*
was not funny in the least, not at all what
they had expected. There was no " ring-round-
rosy," or " button, button," or dancing, or
anything nice. And this was what they called
a wedding !

But it was over before very long, and then
the people began to stir again. There was

a buzz of pleasant talking all through the
room. People here and there laughed softly;
but mamma and one or two other ladies put
their handkerchiefs to their eyes. It couldn't
be that they were crying? How strange!
how very strange! Grown-up ladies crying at
a party!

And people were coming up to kiss Aunt
Vi, and shake hands with Mr. Sanford. What
was that for? If they had only kissed Jimmy
and Lucy, and said how spl-en-didly they
looked, and how well they had behaved, there
might have been some sense in it.

Jimmy's lip curled a little.

And who was *Mrs. Sanford?* Again and
again people went up to Aunt Vi, and said,
" My dear Mrs. Sanford," which of course
wasn't her name.

Then everybody went out to the dining-
room. But think of setting a noble groomsman like Jimmy, and a fair bridesmaid like

Lucy, off in a corner, and telling them to "stay there and not speak yet"!

And before anybody had a chance to eat much, something else happened. Jimmy heard wheels, and, peeping through the window, saw that a carriage had been driven up the gravel path, — a carriage with blue velvet cushions and two handsome chestnut horses.

There it stood and stood. Nobody knew it was there but Jimmy.

And presently Aunt Vi went off in this carriage, and Mr. Sanford went with her. The oddest thing! Right away from the company! So impolite!

Mamma was crying just a little in the hall before they started. Auntie had on a different dress and a new bonnet. She held the children close, and dropped a tear on Lucy's cheek. Poor, poor auntie! how she did hate to go! But Mr. Sanford hurried her into the carriage, which rolled away; and then mamma

and papa went back to the dining-room, and
went on eating chicken-salad.

Up to this time, during all the topsy-turvy
proceedings, people had seemed very cold-
hearted, or very forgetful ; but now they
began to take notice of Jimmy and Lucy.
They said they were the sweetest groomsman
and bridesmaid ever seen, as lovely as fairies ;
and gave them more kisses twice over than
had been given Aunt Vi.

"I dare say this is the first wedding you
ever saw, my love?" asked one of the ladies
of Lucy.

Lucy turned uncertainly to her mother.
"Mamma, did Jimmy and I ever mally anybody before?"

" No, dear."

The children were eating ice-cream now,
their hearts growing every moment happier and
lighter. Still the chief event of the evening
remained a dark mystery.

"What made Aunt Vi go off with Mr. Sanford?" asked the bewildered Jimmy.

Papa replied, —

"Because she loves him best of anybody in
the world."

"Better'n *me*?" said Lucy, looking for her
handkerchief.

The good clergyman tried to explain to his
children that there are many kinds of love
in the world, but all are beautiful and sweet.
Then he talked of Christmas, and of God's
sending his blessed Son to us upon that
day, a little child.

"God's love is best of all," said Mr. Dunlee. "Did you ever fancy for a moment, little
ones, what we should do without our Father's
love?"

"Die, *I* think," replied Jimmy, shivering
and drawing nearer to his little sister. "We
should all cuddle up together and die in a
heap."

But Lucy could talk of nothing but the wedding.

" Auntie never telled me a thing. Did she mally Mr. Sanford 'cause she loved him?"

" To be sure," said Mr. Dunlee.

Lucy drew a quick breath.

" Well, I love my bróther better'n that; I love him 'way up to the moon. Won't you mally me and my brother?"

"Oh, yes," laughed papa. " Put down your cake, and stand up here, both of you."

They stood up. It was a lovely sight as the full light of the chandelier shone down upon them in their bridal array, and turned the hair of both to shining gold.

" I pronounce you brother and sister," said Mr. Dunlee.

And then he laid his hands upon their innocent heads in silent blessing. They did not know what he said, for he said it only to God; but they were both very happy.

"Now you are bound to each other by a chain of love," said mamma, embracing them. "I hope you will be more brotherly, Jimmy-boy, every time you think of it; and I hope you'll be more sisterly, my little Lucy."

"So we've finished off with a wee wedding," said Aunt Jessie Pauly.

And the other guests responded, —

"How beautiful!" and drank healths to "the bonnie wee pair," who were proud to be the centre of notice at last.